KU-159-757

EAST SUSSEX COUNTY COUNCIL
WITHDRAWN
25 OCT 2024
19

# HIRED TO
# WEAR THE
# SHEIKH'S RING

# HIRED TO WEAR THE SHEIKH'S RING

RACHAEL THOMAS

MILLS & BOON

First published in Great Britain 2018
by Mills & Boon, an imprint of HarperCollins*Publishers*
1 London Bridge Street, London, SE1 9GF

Large Print edition 2018



ISBN: 978-0-263-07413-0



This book is produced from independently certified FSC™ paper to ensure responsible forest management.
For more information visit www.harpercollins.co.uk/green.

Printed and bound in Great Britain
by CPI Group (UK) Ltd, Croydon, CR0 4YY

To Joanna Brown, who sowed the seeds of an idea which grew into *Hired to Wear the Sheikh's Ring*.

Thanks!

xx

# CHAPTER ONE

EVERYONE HAD A PRICE. Jafar Al-Shehri knew that better than most. He also knew exactly what that price was as far as bridesmaid Tiffany Chapelle was concerned.

It was a price he was more than prepared to pay in order to get what he wanted. He would do anything to prevent the increasingly hostile claim from his cousin Simdan on the kingdom he'd inherited after his brother's unexpected death. Ruling Shamsumara had never been his ambition, but duty to his people and kingdom, as well as to his brother, was something he would take very seriously. After hearing about Ms Chapelle's unconventional business as a hired bridesmaid, he knew she was exactly what he needed to stave off Simdan's latest attempt to overthrow him.

Jafar's gaze locked with that of the tall slender

woman dressed in a bridesmaid gown of pale blue. She raised her brows in question, then continued with her duties at his friend and business partner Damian Cole's wedding. Her glossy dark brown hair was piled high on her head and dainty white flowers within the style matched the 'English country garden' setting of the wedding. She had a dusting of freckles on her face, which only added to her beauty, to the allure she unwittingly created. The thought of kissing her full lips had remained irritatingly close to the forefront of his mind since they had been introduced as best man and bridesmaid yesterday afternoon at rehearsals.

Ever since she'd smiled up at him, the stunning bridesmaid had unsettled him. He tried to convince himself it was because of the business deal he intended to put to Ms Chapelle and not the sparkling sizzle that had rocketed through him as she'd shook his hand.

When his friend had first announced he was marrying his childhood sweetheart, Jafar hadn't been at all surprised. What had shocked him was that the chief bridesmaid was not a close friend or relative of his bride, but a woman hired to do the job. Tiffany Chapelle made her living from hiring herself to brides as not just a wedding planner, but the chief bridesmaid. Damian had laughed when he'd quizzed him about hiring a stranger, saying every bride should hire their chief bridesmaid, especially if she had overzealous friends like his wife-to-be. Since then, Jafar had done his research on Tiffany thoroughly. Very thoroughly.

She was a woman who appeared to live romance vicariously through other brides' weddings and surprisingly had been hired by many rich and famous names. The fact that she was prepared to hire herself as a bridesmaid made her the perfect candidate for what he had in mind. Added to that, she didn't have any obvious signs of a man in her life but, most importantly for him, she was in considerable debt and had recently given up her rented apartment and moved in with her sister. He hadn't yet discovered what the debt was from but was confident he could strike a deal with her. To him, the debt was nothing and he intended to offer her far more to take on a role that would require her total commitment for the next three months.

The orchestra began to play and Jafar had attended enough Western weddings to know that the bride and groom would now dance alone and that he, as the best man, would be expected to lead the chief bridesmaid to the dance floor to join the happy couple a short time later. His best-man role was a duty he intended to perform with the same exacting standards he did everything, especially as it would give him the opportunity to begin subtle negotiations with the delightful woman fate had delivered into his path as the answer to his problems.

He focused his attention on the bride then his friend. He clenched his teeth together as he watched the commanding man he knew his friend to be, a lethal businessman who took no prisoners, looking adoringly into the eyes of the woman he'd married. He should be happy for Damian but witnessing such devotion, such love, served only to remind him of all he'd lost when he'd discovered Niesha's true colours. They had been promised to one another since they were children and he'd always had a fondness for her that had turned into what he'd then assumed was love. He'd been more than ready to enter into the marriage and make it work. Niesha, however, had set her sights on someone far superior to the spare heir of Shamsumara, as he was then.

The trail of his thoughts led back to his brother and the overwhelming sense of loss for a man who'd been both brother and father to him, shielding him from the wrath of their father's power-hungry ways, which had almost brought the kingdom to its knees. Malek had worked hard to regain the trust of the people and now that duty fell to him. He would not and could not fail his brother.

'I think this is where you come in.' The sultry and somewhat chastising voice of the bridesmaid jilted him from the gathering storm of thoughts as she came to stand next to him.

'I was merely allowing the happy couple time to enjoy the spotlight.' He looked down into blue eyes. They were as pale as her dress but rimmed with deep blue and full of an intensity that did more than hint at her passionate side. That sizzle he'd experienced at yesterday's introduction strengthened, becoming more like a bolt of lightning across the desert sky of his homeland.

Was it excitement at finally being able to put in motion his plan to save the people of his kingdom, Shamsumara, from his cousin's hostile claim on the country that bordered his own? Or was it the thought of being able to hold this particular woman in his arms as they danced?

'And there I was thinking you were avoiding me.' There was a teasing note to her voice, one that suggested a playful nature. A woman who was able to enjoy life.

'I hardly think allowing you time to complete the duties you have been hired for is avoiding you. That is your role, is it not? *Hired* bridesmaid?' His response was swift and the ferocity behind his words surprised him as much as the sizzle of tension around them, but the deal he intended to put to her was far too important to allow himself to be distracted by a pretty face and a sexy figure—or the challenge that lingered in the depths of those sexy eyes.

'You don't approve of me, do you, Mr Al-Shehri?' Her full lips pressed together in annoyance as she stood, one hand on her hip, glaring up at him, her eyes sparking like the icicles he'd always been fascinated with during those long cold winters at boarding school in England. 'Or is it the fact that I charge women to be not only their wedding planner but their bridesmaid too? It may be unconventional but Bridesmaid Services isn't the only business offering such services.'

'Having had the somewhat dubious pleasure of meeting the bride's best friend this afternoon, I can see how there is a need for hiring a bridesmaid who will do all that is required without any dramatics.' He'd soon discovered just what Damian had meant when he'd met the woman in question.

'So it must be me you don't approve of.' She teased him again with a smile and that underlying provocation in her voice, daring him to agree.

Challenge fired in her eyes but, instead of engaging her further in a battle of words, he gently but firmly took her hand from her hip, stifling a smile as her eyes widened in surprise. Before she could protest he led her onto the dance floor, fully aware she had no choice but to do his bidding unless she was prepared to risk drawing unwanted attention to them.

The gathered wedding guests applauded as he pulled her gently towards him, taking her in his arms until he could feel her slender body pressed against his. His body responded instantly to hers, to her scent, light and floral like the classic English garden flowers of the hotel. The movement of her waist beneath his hand as she began to move slowly in time to the music only intensified the surge of lust that hurtled through him.

What the hell was happening? It was as if this dark-haired beauty was sapping his strength, diminishing the control he was renowned for. She was making him want things he'd long ago learnt were not possible. He desired her, of that there was no doubt, but it was much more intense than his usual need of a woman. She was unlocking the man within him who long ago had put aside the need for the companionship of a woman. He knew precisely how destructive needs such as that could be. He shut down the train of thought, banished it from his mind, allowing heated lust to fill his mind and body in its place.

'Are you going to tell me?' The haughty rising of her brows and the challenge in her voice helped to snap him from the edge of somewhere he hadn't been for a long time. Somewhere he had no wish to venture ever again—memories of his past, of the life he could have led with the young girl he'd grown up with, the woman who should have become his bride. He pushed them savagely away. Now was not the time to complicate the future with the past and what he'd hoped for.

'It is not that I disapprove of you,' he said softly, holding her gaze as other couples now joined them on the dance floor. 'Quite the reverse.'

'You approve?' There was genuine shock in those lovely eyes now and despite the memories she'd almost cracked open he laughed softly.

'I do, yes.' He smiled at her increasing shock. 'You are the first woman I have met who doesn't attach sentimental nonsense to a wedding.'

She tilted her head to one side and looked up at him, her eyes narrowing slightly with suspicion. 'This is my job, Mr Al-Shehri. I am merely doing what I have been hired to do, which is to make it the best day of the bride's life.'

'So your sense of duty is strong?' He engaged willingly in the conversation, pleased that he could discover all the finer details about this woman from her, not second-hand through someone else. Private investigators could only glean so much, but they could never inform him of what made a person tick and it was important he got all the answers he needed before he put his deal to her. A deal that would secure his kingdom, Shamsumara, and maybe even set to rest the ghosts of his past once and for all.

'I'm dancing with you, aren't I?' Laughter sparked in her eyes and even though he wanted to keep their discussion on track and on a businesslike footing, he couldn't help but laugh too.

'I had no idea it would be such an arduous task for you.' He propelled them to the edge of the dance floor and towards the exit from the grand marquee, decked out in white and pale pink. The flower arrangements were all of the same white and pink flowers; only the bridesmaids in pale blue deviated from the colour scheme. 'Shall we enjoy the late-afternoon sunshine?'

'Are you taking me away from my duties, Mr Al-Shehri?' She was testing him, of that there was no doubt.

Jafar glanced at Damian and his bride, dancing as if they were one being. 'I think your duties are over for now. The bride and groom look blissfully unaware of anything except each other.'

Tiffany didn't miss the undertone of steely irritation in the best man's accented voice. All day she'd felt his gaze on her. She'd been acutely aware of him since their first meeting yesterday, in a way that unsettled her, tugging at dreams of love and happiness she'd long since given up on. As she'd sizzled beneath his scrutiny she had tried hard to ignore the disapproving set of his mouth, which had only increased each time they'd had to spend any amount of time together.

She'd also tried to ignore the fact that he was extremely handsome, tall and, with his dark skin, had an exotic appeal she knew had captured the attention of many female guests at the wedding—married and single alike. If circumstances were different, if she weren't here to work, then maybe he would be just the distraction from life she needed right now. Shocked at the direction her thoughts had wandered, she forced herself back to the present, wishing her best friend, Lilly, hadn't planted the idea of a casual fling, a one-night stand, as the best way to rid herself of the bad memories of her ex-boyfriend. She just wasn't that kind of girl. That was why she'd been dumped.

'Now I do detect a note of cynicism,' she said as she looked up at him, shielding her eyes from the glare of the late-afternoon summer sun with her hand as they stopped at the edge of the rose terrace. It was obvious this man was as against the idea of marriage as she now was but it was men like him who had shattered her illusion of true love.

'Do you believe in love and happiness, Miss Chapelle?' His gaze pierced hers and the vivid green of his eyes was in total contrast to his inky black hair and not at all what she'd expected when she'd been told the best man was a desert sheikh, ruler of a kingdom far away.

Tiffany reeled at the direct question, at his scathing tone. It proved her thoughts of moments ago—he most certainly didn't. She also was well aware of his reputation with women after listening to the bride chatter with the other three bridesmaids, all of whom were friends and one very obviously smitten with the dark desert stranger.

'As a matter of fact, I don't.' She pushed back her long-held dreams of finding the kind of love her parents had never managed to, standing taller in the face of this man's challenge. 'Not that I would ever let any bride I work with know that.'

He looked into her eyes, the connection so intense she could hardly breathe, but she wouldn't give him the satisfaction of looking away, of fluttering her eyelashes and enticing him to make her his next conquest. She almost gasped at the thought. What on earth made her think a man like him would want anything to do with her, a woman who, at the age of twenty-five, was yet to experience the touch of a man's caress and the pleasure of that ultimate intimacy between a man and woman? She'd been adamant she wanted to wait until her wedding night, until she'd found that fairy-tale happy ending.

'I like you, Miss Chapelle.' He turned from her, leaving her visibly weak after being under the spotlight of his gaze, but his next words sent her back into the spiral of confusion he'd had her in since he'd taken her hand and led her to the dance floor. 'I think it's important to like the person you are married to.'

She looked at his broad shoulders, encased in the dark charcoal-grey suit he wore, and wondered why such a self-assured, bordering on arrogant man couldn't face her and say the words.

She touched a nearby pink rose, the softness of its petals strangely calming. 'Yes, I think you are right. After all, if you don't like the person you marry, the odds of the marriage lasting are pretty slim.'

Her parents were testament to that. As were the arguments followed by stony silence she'd grown up thinking were normal. It was only when they'd split up and she'd been old enough to stay over at friends' that she'd realised it was far from normal. Those volatile early years of her life had made her resolute in her determination that she would have a happy, love-filled marriage.

He turned to face her. 'We agree on that, at least.'

'We do?' He confused her, one minute talking as if referring to marriage and friendship in general, then as if the discussion were directly related to them. As if they were a couple about to be married.

'Indeed, yes.' He moved towards her and the scent of his aftershave, exotic and wild, hit her as it had done on the dance floor. At least this time she wasn't pressed against his body, feeling every move he made, igniting sensations—hot, burning sensations—she'd never felt before. 'And therefore I would like to engage your services.'

'You're getting married.' She couldn't keep the shock from her voice. This man was a playboy desert sheikh who made no secret of the many women he'd loved and left. She'd found that out very easily when she'd looked him up on the Internet, just as she always did with every best man she was paired with. At least then she was able to find out the type of man he was, but Sheikh Jafar Al-Shehri had surpassed every other best man she'd worked alongside. Ruler of a desert kingdom, a reformed playboy prince after unexpectedly inheriting the title, he was the ultimate incarnation of everything she wanted to avoid in a man.

He was also everything she'd been searching for in a man, yet had never expected to find. Ever since her only steady boyfriend had dumped her because she'd wanted to wait until they were married to share intimacies, she'd been very cautious about getting involved again. The idea that the desert sheikh could be the man to have a wild, passionate one-night stand with in order to shake off her past, as her friend Lilly had put it, was a step too far.

'I am.' His deep and commanding voice crashed through her wild train of thoughts, bringing her sharply back to the present. How could she be having such thoughts about this man?

She forced herself to look into those sexy eyes, to appear in control even though her heart began to thump harder in her chest. Was it his sudden closeness or her thoughts? 'And you want me to organise your wedding and be bridesmaid to your bride?'

He looked at her, assessing her; an air of calculation lingered around them. 'No, I want to hire you—as my bride.'

She blinked and looked up at him, unable to say anything, then to her utter embarrassment she laughed.

Jafar inhaled deeply and waited while the prim and proper Miss Chapelle's laughter subsided.

How dared she laugh at him? Nobody but his closest friends would dare to do such a thing. Didn't she know who he was?

'I think you have had too much champagne, Mr Al-Shehri.' Her voice still rang with laughter and a smile twitched at the edges of his mouth as she teased him, showing him a light-hearted side to her he found intriguing, but he forced it down.

'I am in full and total control,' he said as he prepared to play his ultimate ace. 'I have need of a bride and you, I believe, have need of a large sum of money to cover debts.'

Silence sliced between them as she looked at him suspiciously, all trace of laughter suddenly gone. The dark rims of blue around her eyes reminding him of the ocean that formed one border to his kingdom, but the paler centres had become hostile, like the heat of the desert. 'I see I am not the only one to have been doing some research.'

The tartness of her voice warned him he was pushing her too far but, as ever, the challenge of getting *exactly* what he wanted pushed him on. 'I never enter into anything, not even being a best man to my childhood friend, without doing my research, Miss Chapelle.'

'So, do enlighten me, what has your research turned up?' She folded her right arm across her, beneath her breasts, placing the elbow of the other arm in her hand. Then, in a sexily tormenting gesture, she placed her thumb under her chin and her finger on her lips, sending a bolt of hot desire surging through him.

Her eyes blazed like the purest of gems, and her full lips snagged his attention as a bright red fingernail pushed into their plumpness. The late-afternoon sunlight danced in her hair, turning it to fiery bronze, highlighting the freckles sprinkled over her face. All he could think about was pulling her hard against his body, pressing her curves into him and kissing her. There was nothing gentle about the heat in his body, the need to touch her, kiss her, possess her. Without a doubt, he knew that if he gave in to the demands of his body now, it would be fierce, savage and wild. It would be total possession and if he weren't putting such an outlandish deal to her, he might already be taking her to his suite here in the hotel.

'I think you are bluffing, Mr Al-Shehri.' Her words dragged him from the erotic images of just what he'd like to do to her, sharply focusing his attention once more.

'You are in debt and you also need more, much more, thanks to your brother-in-law, who has left your sister in a very precarious financial situation.' He'd discovered that useful bit of information at almost the eleventh hour.

She gasped, her eyes becoming wide with shock. 'How do you know that?'

'I made it my business to know, Miss Chapelle.' He moved towards her, unintentionally breathing in her delicate scent, serving only to stir his body's needs once more. 'Everybody has a price and I now know yours.'

'So you want to pay me to be your bride?'

'Yes, Miss Chapelle, I do.' He'd just heard Damian say those words to his bride, but they'd been said with love, with hope for the future. Now he was saying them to this woman who stirred his senses in a way no other woman had; even Niesha, the woman he should have married if his life hadn't careered off course, hadn't ever roused in him such intense passion.

'And what makes you think I would agree to such a bizarre request?' Both her arms were folded protectively in front of her now, one hand pulling firmly on the other arm, serving only to press her breasts together in a way the pale blue dress couldn't disguise. Lust throbbed through him but he pushed it aside. This was not one of his casual affairs; this was a woman who held the future of his kingdom in her hands. The answer she gave him decided the fate of his people—and his.

If she declined, then his cousin, Simdan, would have every right to challenge his ability to rule. He didn't have the time to find a wife in the conventional way of his country. Besides, with his sister expecting her first child, which he intended to name as his heir, he didn't require a wife, merely a bride.

'As I intend our marriage to take place in two

weeks' time you will be financially rewarded and therefore able to settle all your debts, and those of your sister. I will also ensure you have a substantial amount of money once our agreement is complete.'

'No,' she said, shaking her head. 'I have absolutely no intention of getting married for any sum of money and certainly not in two weeks.'

Jafar hadn't expected her to say yes instantly. Indeed, he would have worried that she saw him as some kind of knight in shining armour, the answer to a woman's dreams of happy ever afters, if she had. But in light of her current financial situation, he hadn't expected an outright no.

'So what has happened to the bridesmaid who ensures a bride's dream comes true to make her so against marriage?' He taunted her and satisfaction filled him as he saw her visible blanch at his question. It seemed she too had issues with the state of matrimony.

'What makes you sure something has happened?' She flung the question straight back at him.

'A woman who prefers to always be the bridesmaid and not the bride is definitely hiding from something.' He resisted the urge to tuck a stray strand of hair behind her ear as it slipped from the confines of her bridal hairdo, but had to clench his fist tightly in order to do that.

'This is my job, Mr Al-Shehri.' She glared at him and once again the need to kiss away the angry tension in those lips lurched forwards. 'Only a man like you could seriously contemplate buying a bride.'

Irritation spiked at the desire. She dared to challenge him? 'And what kind of man is that, Miss Chapelle?'

Tiffany could hardly contain her anger. How dared he offer to buy her? What kind of country did he rule over if he thought he could simply buy a bride when the need arose? Even worse than that, she had actually contemplated accepting because right now she'd do anything to free her sister, Bethany, of that abusive, gambling man she'd married seven years ago, and sort out the financial mess he'd created then walked away and left her in.

'The kind of man who can buy just about anything he wants, even, it seems, a bride.' She hurled the accusation at him and turned quickly, intent on walking away from him, from the lure of the answer to Bethany's financial problems and the almost irresistible draw of the man himself.

'Can you really afford to walk away from such an offer?' His words were hard and full of determination. Her steps faltered and she stood with her back to him, breathing deeply, still shocked by the way being close to him had made her feel as well as the outrageous proposition he'd put to her. 'Can you really deny your sister?'

She whirled round. 'I have no idea how you have managed to find out so much about me and my family, Mr Al-Shehri, but I will not be bought.'

He moved towards her, his long strides closing the gap between them. 'I have no intention of buying *you*, Miss Chapelle. I merely wish to hire you to accompany me to Shamsumara and become my bride. Beyond that we can remain exactly as we are. Strangers.'

'Your audacity almost makes me speechless,' she hurled at him. 'You even expect me to go to your country.'

'I doubt there is much that can make you speechless.' The tormenting laughter in his voice was clear, and as he smiled and raised his brows at her she wanted to stamp her foot and scream in frustration, but before she could do anything he continued the onslaught. 'Just as I know you will do anything you can for your sister—and her little girl.'

Now he'd hit her Achilles heel. Four-year-old Kelly didn't deserve to be caught up in the mess her parents had created. The acrimonious divorce had turned her from a bright happy child to an anxious little girl who barely spoke and Tiffany would do absolutely anything to rectify that, especially as she knew what it felt like to be that little girl.

'This has nothing to do with my niece.' She

could barely control her anger now. How dared he bring an innocent child into this absurd deal?

'Think about it, Tiffany.' The sound of her name on his lips shocked her, not least because of the dart of pleasure it sent coursing through her. 'Meet me here after breakfast tomorrow, when I am sure you will have come to realise this deal is the answer to all your problems.'

## CHAPTER TWO

TIFFANY HAD TOSSED and turned all night, the usual buzz of having created another perfect day for a bride obliterated by Sheikh Jafar Al-Shehri's outrageous suggestion. It wasn't any kind of normal contract. He didn't want a bridesmaid. He wanted a *bride*. He wanted to buy her and that had unsettled her almost as much as the reaction of her body whenever he was close. Not to mention the steamy images, which had raced into her mind, of being kissed by him. A kiss she instinctively knew would be earth-shattering and dangerous.

As dawn had crept into the room she'd given up on sleep and left her hotel room and gone for a walk. It always helped to clear her mind and by the time she returned she knew she would accept the deal—but on her terms.

She changed into a short black summer dress and slipped on her black leather jacket, the only other outfit she had with her other than jeans and jumper, not having expected to have to be negotiating any kind of deal this morning. She made her way to the terrace with purpose in her step, intent on putting to him her terms for acceptance of his deal. The morning air was fragrant with roses but there was no sign of the man himself. She looked at her watch. She was late and she guessed he was the kind of man who didn't tolerate tardy timekeeping. A flutter of panic threatened. This was the chance she needed, and probably the only one she'd get, to make things right for Bethany and Kelly, and she'd thrown it away.

She turned to check she hadn't missed him. Not that anyone could miss noticing a man like that. With a flash of relief she saw Sheikh Jafar Al-Shehri striding across the terrace, the morning sunlight behind him as he came towards her. Just as she expected, he was dressed immaculately in a suit that had definitely been made for him if the way it hugged his long legs, hips and shoulders was anything to go by. Handsome didn't even go halfway to describing him. Sexy was the word that came to mind, but she slammed it back, refusing to accept she was in any way attracted to him.

'Good morning,' she said brightly, as if meeting with a man to thrash out the finer details of a marriage contract were something she did every day.

'Would you like to walk or have coffee?' His fiercely alert gaze travelled down her, taking in the dress, which was probably too short to meet with a man who ruled a desert kingdom, finally resting on her white high-heeled sandals.

Again she'd earnt his disapproval. 'I'm not really dressed for walking. Coffee would be better.'

'Indeed,' he said as he gestured with an outstretched hand that she should precede him to the tables outside set for breakfast.

A thrill of something she'd never known before skipped up her spine as she became acutely aware of his eyes on her. The intensity of his scrutiny burned through her leather jacket and the fine fabric of the dress, making her shiver as if she were cold. In contrast the kind of heat from sipping fine brandy flooded through her.

As they neared the terrace of the restaurant a member of staff appeared instantly, eager to please the sheikh, and she realised for the first time just what his life must be like. He was much wealthier than any of the couples she had been hired by in the past, although plenty of them had given her a window into the world of wealth and luxury. This man, however, far surpassed that.

'A quiet table for two.' He spoke firmly, demanding precisely what he wanted without so much as a please or thank you.

'This way, Sheikh Al-Shehri.' The waiter led them to a secluded table at the edge of the terrace, where a mass of climbing roses clung to a trellis forming the perfect private area. The view from the table across the rolling English landscape was unrivalled, but, with her nerves like that of a young colt, she wasn't in the mood to appreciate it.

Tiffany allowed herself to be seated, as if waiting for such a thing were normal, and then tried to focus her attention on the view instead of the formidably brooding presence of the man she was about to strike the most bizarre deal with. A deal that, given the imminent repossession of Bethany's home, was now the only option she had.

'I'll come straight to the point, Mr Al-Shehri.' She paused for a moment to gather herself as he fixed his attention on her, wanting to word this right, but before she could say any more he filled that pause.

'Decisive. That is good. I like a woman who knows what she wants.' She looked at him, into those green eyes, and wondered if he was mocking her, but there wasn't even the smallest hint of a smile. In fact there was very little trace of any emotion. Only severe control.

She began again before her nerve failed her. 'Providing my terms are met, I will accept your deal. I will be your hired bride.'

Those last two words almost choked her. After the mess and complications of her parents' divorce, she'd longed to find true love and happiness. Her ex-boyfriend hadn't understood her need to wait to take their relationship to the next level and now she accepted her reluctance to do so was because she hadn't loved him. Not in the deep and intense way she'd always dreamt it would be when she met the man she would spend the rest of her life with.

'Terms?' He sat back, his elbow resting on the arm of the chair, his thumb and finger moving over his chin, the subtle sound of the hint of dark stubble snagging her attention.

'Yes, my terms,' she fired back at him, defiantly lifting her chin, determined to stand up for herself. 'You didn't think I would just accept whatever conditions you put forward, did you?'

'Very well.' He folded his arms across his chest and fixed her with the searing heat of his gaze and an explosion of fire erupted within her. 'What are your terms?'

This time there was a hint of amusement in his voice, the slightest movement upwards of his lips. She almost laughed out loud when she realised he'd probably never had anyone set out their terms to him for anything. He must be used to getting precisely what he wanted all the time. Well, she wasn't about to make this easy for him. Yes, she needed the money, and needed it now, but she had to keep some dignity, had to demand at least something for herself. After all, marrying anyone was a big deal, let alone a stranger.

'Before we discuss that, I want to know why you need a bride in such a hurry and why me?' She looked at him, using the fire to boost her confidence, to show him she was a woman who could hold her own. 'Why not a woman from your country? In fact, I think you are hiding something, Mr Al-Shehri.'

'Jafar,' he said calmly. Completely unruffled by her questions. 'I'd much prefer to be on first-name terms with the woman I am negotiating a marriage contract with. It's so much more personal, don't you agree?'

Her fierce response to that question was halted by the arrival of coffee and for a moment she allowed herself to believe this wasn't happening, that none of this was real as the strong aroma of coffee fired her senses.

'Well?' he demanded as they were once more left alone. 'Do you agree, Tiffany?'

The emphasis he put into her name, his exotic accent caressing every syllable, made her pulse leap and she had to force herself to look into his eyes, to meet the power of this man head-on without flinching, without showing any fear or doubt. 'Absolutely, Jafar.'

His name seemed strangely familiar to her tongue as she sat straight and tall in the chair in a bid to appear as in control as he was. She almost achieved that until he smiled. It happened so suddenly she quite literally forgot to breathe as she became the focus of his attention. Heat sizzled over her at an alarming rate.

Jafar watched as a charming blush bloomed on Tiffany's cheeks, knocking the confident businesswoman sideways and allowing him to glimpse the woman he believed she never wanted him to find. The passionate, yet shy woman who lived beneath her toughened exterior. That was precisely why he wouldn't be giving in to the urge to kiss her that he'd had since the moment they had been introduced. She was wrong for him on so many levels, but right in only one. She needed him as much as he needed her, not that he'd ever allow her to know just how much.

'What exactly do you want to know, Tiffany?' She looked at him, then away, that shyness coming to the fore once more. It intrigued him. Maybe the time they would have to be together as man and wife was going to be far more interesting than he'd anticipated.

'Why a man such as yourself has to marry a complete stranger within two weeks?' Her blunt question fired directly at him and he admired her honesty, even if it meant he would have to share part of himself, part of his past with her. Something he never did with women.

He looked away across the fields of green grass as he thought of his brother, Malek, and the accident that had claimed him and his wife. That tragic day had made Jafar the ruler of Shamsumara. He'd always had the good of the country at heart, but never once in recent years, when he'd been sharing the burden of bringing the kingdom back to a good place to live after the tough years his father had ruled with hardness and cruelty, had he imagined himself the ruler. Jafar had never considered the possibility that one day that responsibility would lie solely with him.

'I became the ruler of the kingdom of Shamsumara after a sudden family death. One which has left the country in a vulnerable position, open to the challenge of leadership from a man who rules his own kingdom with the same fear and dominance my father had ruled with. It is not the way I rule and I will not allow my people to live through that again.'

He looked at her face, saw the confusion in her eyes and knew this must be sounding so far-fetched to her. A dart of doubt shot through him. Was he doing the right thing, involving this woman in the affairs of his country? She might be in need of the sort of funds he could easily provide, but would she be able to fulfil the duties that would be required of her as his Queen? Even if it was only for a short time?

'It seems to me that you need far more than a bride,' she said as she sipped her coffee. He looked at his, but knew he wouldn't taste it, that the memory of his brother and the threat posed by his cousin, the one man he truly hated, would obliterate all sense of taste. 'You need a wife, a *proper* wife, a woman to give you heirs. That woman would be your Queen, wouldn't she?'

He couldn't help the shock that slammed into him. Maybe he'd misjudged this alluring woman. She was far more astute than he'd given her credit for. 'Yes, my bride will be my Queen and in normal terms an heir is exactly what I would need, but, on this occasion, no. My sister married last year and is expecting her first child. The usual order of things in our country is that *her* child will become my heir until such a time as I have my own child, which of course I don't plan to do. So producing an heir myself isn't necessary.'

She narrowed her eyes at him. 'I'm confused. If

you don't need an heir why not marry a woman from your own country?'

'Because I have no wish to be married in the true sense of the word.' How the hell did he put the last two years into a few concise sentences that would make sense to her? 'As an unmarried ruler, I am open to challenge. That challenge would come from my cousin Simdan, who rules harshly over a small country which borders Shamsumara. He wants my kingdom for the power it would bring him—and the wealth. Shamsumara is rich in oil.'

'And if you were married?' The question lingered in the air like the threat of thunder.

'My cousin has recently become a father and as a married ruler with an heir he can challenge my rule. If I married, his immediate ability to challenge me would become less and once my sister's child is born and declared my heir, his claim on my throne is no longer valid.'

She put down her coffee cup with a clatter, spilling the dark liquid into the saucer. 'When is the baby due?'

'At the end of October.' It was this very fact and the possibility that things could even now go wrong in his sister's pregnancy that necessitated Jafar's marriage. He was well aware that Simdan was already making moves to launch a claim for Shamsumara. If the unthinkable happened and his sister lost her baby, he would at least be the married ruler tradition demanded.

'So where exactly do I come into all this?' The panic in her voice was clear and he quickly realised where his explanation had taken her thoughts.

'I only require you to be my bride. I have no intention of making a real marriage or having my own children, not when my nephew or niece will soon be born.' He saw those expressive eyes widen and knew exactly what she was thinking. Three months was a long time and anything could happen. It was his aide's main concern too.

'If that is the case, why do you need to marry at all?' Was that a hint of relief he detected in her voice? She pushed her coffee cup away as if the conversation was coming to an end, as if she'd already decided she would not take him up on the deal. He couldn't allow that. He had much to lose and so did she. Something he would remind her of. 'Can't you name the baby now as your heir?'

'In order to continue to rule in my brother's place I must be married the day after the feast of Shams, which is two weeks from now, or my cousin has every right to claim the kingdom.' Just as she had done yesterday, she laughed. He bit down hard against the irritation. How dared she when her own life was in such a mess? 'I must then remain for two years.'

'Two years?'

'You would only be required to remain in Shamsumara as my wife and Queen for three months or until my sister's baby is born. We will have to remain legally married for two years, but after that a divorce will be easy to procure. And, of course, you will have a very substantial settlement.'

'And because of my job and my financial situation you thought I would be desperate enough to be your hired bride?' The amusement in her voice held no malice but it didn't soften his mood. He was not used to having to cajole women around to his way of thinking.

'I would rate imminent repossession of your sister's home desperate, but, of course, if you don't…' He left the sentence unfinished, his withdrawal of the deal, which he knew full well she needed, hang in the morning air between them. It felt like the biggest gamble he'd ever made. She looked at him in silence, something other than strained tension zapping between them. Raw desire.

'I find it alarming that you know so much about me, Mr Al-Shehri.' The curtness of her tone when she finally spoke left him in no doubt he'd touched a raw nerve.

'I thought we were on more informal terms now, Tiffany.' He added her name, enjoying the flash of anger in the depths of her eyes. He leant forward in his chair and lowered his voice. 'We are, after all, almost engaged.'

'Not so fast. Not until you have agreed to my terms—all of them.' He admired the fire of defiance burning within her, revelled in the challenge she was unwittingly creating. He thrived on challenge, hated meek-willed individuals who would agree to anything he said just because of who he was.

At last he'd met a woman who was more than a match for him. The next three months of living as man and wife would prove very interesting indeed. 'I think it's about time you told me just what they are.'

She sat back as she looked at him, the haughty lift of her chin showing her spirit, reminding him of an unbroken horse. She had as much spirit as a stallion and, just as he did with his horses, he looked forward to harnessing that spirit, to turning her into one of his graceful falcons that would fly at his bequest and return willingly to his arm.

The thought shocked him. Did he want a woman to return to him, to want to be with him? It was something he'd never sought before so why now? Because she would be his wife, his hired bride?

'First of all I want a payment up front. Today.' She looked at him, as if waiting for his objection, but he merely sat and studied her. 'I want a quarter of a million pounds in my account before the end of the day and a second payment the day we marry.'

Was that all? He'd planned on offering her much more than that. 'Consider that done. Anything else?'

Tiffany looked at Jafar, at the handsome and very regal figure he cut sitting opposite her. Had he really agreed to that amount of money without so much as a flicker of a reaction? Was he that used to buying everything he needed he didn't care what it cost?

She still couldn't believe that by her simply agreeing to stand beside this man and become his wife, all Bethany's problems would be over. It was almost too good to be true. The saying of looking a gift horse in the mouth drifted through her mind as she looked at the firm line of his full lips. Was it really going to be this easy to help her sister and secure a future for her niece, Kelly?

'I will need to continue my business.' His frown slashed her confidence and her words stalled.

'You have other bridesmaid contracts such as yesterday's?'

She hadn't taken any bookings for the next six weeks because Kelly was about to finish nursery school for summer holidays. It was her chance to give Bethany a break and really be there for Kelly as she prepared to start big girl school in September. It was also a reminder that being an aunt could well be the closest she'd ever come to being a mother herself, with her dreams of finding true love and a happy marriage sabotaged by this man's deal. She would put aside her dream for her sister and niece because she could never be happy knowing she'd walked away from the only chance to sort things out for them.

'The next wedding is booked for early September and I will need to visit the bride between now and then.'

'You will remain in Shamsumara for the full three months specified unless I accompany you.' The harshness of his tone shouldn't have surprised her, but it did. She was helping him out as much as he was helping her. Maybe it was time to remind him of that.

'In that case you will have to do exactly that.'

'No, that is out of the question.'

She pushed her chair back and stood up, slowly and full of poise and dignity. 'In that case, Mr Al-Shehri, we will not be able to strike a deal.' She was calling his bluff and he damn well knew it, but she didn't care. This was her stand. If he'd managed to find out all about Bethany's financial situation, then he knew just how desperate she was, but there was no way she would ever act it in front of him.

'I don't think for one minute you intend to walk away from this deal.' The vibrancy of his eyes pierced into her, dragging her secrets from the depths she'd hidden them. 'And while I do applaud your honour to your business commitments I insist you stay in Shamsumara for three months. My cousin must see our marriage as real if it is to achieve its objective.'

'And what does that mean?' Irrational anger

bubbled away within her like a hot spring. 'I can't continue my business? That I can't return to England and make arrangements for my client?'

'It means that you can continue with your business but I would prefer you to remain in Shamsumara. How many other weddings do you have to attend to?' There was a brittle harshness in his tone, which only served to anger her further.

'There are others in later months, but our three-month deal will be over by then and no concern of yours.' His brows rose at her tone and that sexy hint of a smile made her tummy somersault and to hide her embarrassment she sat back down, wondering if Bethany could stand in for her and visit her client.

'As it is just the one client, then I am happy to support that.' There was a mischievous glint in his eyes and she wondered if he was toying with her, but now was not the time to test it out. She needed that incredible sum of money he was prepared to pay if she was going to secure Bethany's and Kelly's future, keep a roof over their heads. She'd even be able to set herself up once this bizarre marriage was over and three months wasn't that long.

'In that case, Mr Al-Shehri, we have a deal.' She stood up and put her hand out to shake on the deal. He stood and looked down at her, then finally took her hand in his, but not in the way she'd expected. He held her fingertips and lifted her hand to his lips, his gaze locked on hers all the time, and then kissed the backs of her fingers.

The spark of fire that kiss evoked rushed up her arm, making her heart flutter as if she were a teenager. Shyness crept over her and she lowered her lashes, blocking out the intensity of his eyes.

'I will send my car for you next Friday.' If she didn't know any better she'd say that the moment had affected him too, his voice was more of a hoarse whisper, but surely not. A playboy sheikh who had the pick of all the glamorous women he wanted would never be affected by a woman like her. Did he have any idea just how inexperienced she was with such things? 'Is that sufficient time for you to put things in order?'

Put things in order. Could that ever really be

achieved? At least the payment he'd agreed on would take away the threat of repossession for her sister.

'Yes, perfectly sufficient,' she said, keeping her voice brisk and businesslike, trying not to think of the implications of accepting his proposal. After all, it wasn't a real proposal and certainly wouldn't be a real marriage.

'Good, then it is settled. You will accompany me to Paris, where we shall make it obvious to anyone who sees us that we are not only a couple in love, but engaged to be married.' His bold confidence almost knocked hers, but she held her ground, kept her composure.

'If arranged marriages are acceptable in your country, why do we need to do that?'

'Because this is not a conventional arrangement and I do not wish to give anyone, least of all my cousin, the chance to challenge it. We will act out our engagement in Paris for one week. In private I will instruct you on all you need to know and provide you with everything necessary for your role. After that we will travel to Shamsumara and arrive in time for the feast of Shams—and our wedding ceremony.'

'So soon?' The hesitation in her voice brought his scrutiny to her once more.

'I trust you are not getting cold feet?'

'Absolutely not. This is a deal that will enable us both to get what we want and for my sister and her daughter I will go to Paris with you, then to your country to become your wife.'

## CHAPTER THREE

FIVE DAYS LATER Tiffany was waiting for the car Jafar had told her would collect her. She had put her life in order, at least as much as she possibly could, given the bizarre deal she'd agreed to. She pushed the implications of marriage to a man like Jafar Al-Shehri to the back of her mind as a sleek black and very luxurious-looking car pulled up outside her sister's house. At least Bethany wasn't here to try one last time to talk her out of it, having left early to go with Kelly on her nursery school trip.

Tiffany took hold of the handle of her suitcase and looked around the living room one last time. Kelly's toys, as usual, were scattered around everywhere and the book Bethany was reading was face down on the coffee table. Shock crashed over Tiffany like angry waves. She wouldn't be here to see the book finished or the toys played with. She would be in a country she barely knew anything about, married to a man she knew even less about.

Was she doing the right thing?

'Stop it,' she berated herself. It wasn't as if she'd be away for ever. Just three months. She had to do this, for Bethany and Kelly, and there wasn't really any other option left to them. With a determinedly inhaled breath, she turned and walked out of the house to the waiting car, its darkened windows making it impossible to see inside.

The driver's door opened and Jafar got out. The burst of determination that had filled her just moments ago vanished as his eyes met hers. He looked sexy and incredibly powerful. The black suit, over which he wore an expensive camel-coloured coat to ward off the unusual chill in the summer air, only elevated his aura of command.

A skitter of apprehension raced down her spine, excitement hot in pursuit. How could just one look from this man have such a profound effect on her? 'I wasn't expecting you.'

The words were out before she could stop them or give herself the chance to act as calmly and in control as he so effortlessly did. He remained tall and straight as he stood next to the car.

'We have much to do once we arrive in Paris before we begin the act of a whirlwind romance.' There was a new depth to his voice. Was it more command or more determination?

She moved closer to the car and as he came to take her case from her she could see the determination in his eyes too. The fierce spark of power that only a man in complete control of his destiny could have.

*He's also in control of your destiny and will be for the next two years.*

'Such as?' she demanded fiercely as that thought lingered in her mind like the ash after a fire.

It was the first time she'd thought beyond the three months he had stipulated she spend in his country. She'd been so wrapped up in being able to help Bethany she hadn't thought of what would happen for the remainder of their so-called marriage and it was now one of the things she intended to sort out in Paris.

Jafar opened the passenger door for her and stood looking down at her. Was it possible that he suddenly seemed taller than she remembered or was it because she was losing control rapidly? She could still back out. She looked at the house she'd moved into with Bethany and Kelly several months ago and knew she couldn't, not if she wanted to help them keep a roof over their heads, and now that Bethany knew all about this deal she definitely couldn't.

She met the suspicion in his eyes and spoke again before he had a chance to say anything. 'All the trimmings that come with such a whirlwind romance?'

'One thing you will learn about me, Tiffany, is that if I do something, I do it properly.' He paused and stepped a fraction closer so that she caught the exotic scent of his aftershave. It was wild and free, like the air itself—or the desert. As she tried to halt those thoughts he spoke again. 'And making you my wife will be no exception.'

No response to that statement came to mind and instead she got into the car, trying to ignore the sensation of overwhelming wealth and luxury that assaulted her senses as she did so as wildly as the man himself. Jafar got into the driver's seat and soon they were heading towards London for their flight to Paris. She watched the countryside she'd grown up in rush past, her thoughts crammed with just how he was going to make their engagement and subsequent marriage appear real. She was thankful when music began to play gently against the hum of the car engine. She forced her mind to relax, to go with the absurd deal she'd struck with this man. A man who had the ability to make her wish for things she'd vowed never to want. He made her want to be desired and even loved.

The full extent of the contract she would sign with the desert sheikh became apparent later that day, as she entered the suite of one of Paris's most prestigious hotels to find the room full of designer dresses, shoes, handbags. Everything the kind of woman she was expected to be could want.

'Now I am beginning to understand what you said to me earlier.' She was determined to keep the complete shock and wonderment from her voice. There was no way she was going to allow him to know he was playing into the kind of Cinderella moment almost every girl dreamt of. 'You certainly seem intent on kitting me out properly.'

'As I have said, we need to be seen having a whirlwind affair while we are here in Paris and you need to look the part.'

This was confirmation that she was not at all like the kind of woman he usually associated with. She didn't have the experience of men like him to start with. What if he realised that and backed out of their deal? She couldn't allow that to happen. She would have to ensure she played her part well, be what he wanted her to be.

'I had all this arranged.' He gestured around him at the rails of clothes. 'To provide you with all you will need.'

His deep voice was silky, his words gentle, but there was no mistaking the undertone of icy determination in them. Or the accusation that she was far from suitable and it hurt. For some strange reason it mattered to Tiffany what this man thought of her. She hid her confusion at that revelation behind sharp-edged words.

'If I am so very unsuitable, then why are we even doing this?' She couldn't help but test him, push him to the limits.

She saw his jaw clench as he looked at her from across the luxurious surroundings he was so obviously used to. 'Our arrangement serves us both well. I am in need of a wife and you are in need of money, part of which you have already received.'

'You make it sound so cold.' He glared at her and she hid the smile of satisfaction that she had riled him, rattled his gilded cage a little.

'Not getting sentimental on me, are you?' He moved closer to her, his steps silenced by the thick carpet of the room. Now he was testing her.

She could feel his presence invading her, feel him taking over the very air she breathed. 'No way.' She lifted her chin to look into those fierce eyes and tried to ignore the jolt of something unidentifiable, yet exceedingly powerful, that zapped through her as if he had actually touched her. 'This is merely another contract as far as I am concerned.'

'Good.' The word was strong, forceful. 'I wouldn't want you to get the wrong idea when I begin to wine and dine you and act like a lover who wants nothing more than to seduce you.'

She swallowed hard against the sizzle that held both fear and excitement as images raced into her mind of this man doing exactly that. 'You are not my type, Mr Al-Shehri. There is no need to worry about that.'

The fire in her voice sent a thunderbolt of lust-filled desire streaking through him. Tiffany Chapelle was as good as issuing him a challenge. The challenge of seducing her and right at this moment it was all he could think of doing. He wanted her naked beneath him as she writhed in ecstasy, begging him for more.

A knock on the hotel-suite door hammered through him as if he'd been slapped in the face. What the hell was he thinking, wanting this woman? All he needed to do was marry her, make her his wife in name only and then live with her for three months. Once his sister's child was born, they could return to their lives and divorce in two years' time. If he made love to her, either before or after they were married, it would turn their deal into something so much more. Not to mention harder to extricate himself from.

'Come,' he snapped as the control began to return to his body, even though his mind still reeled with images of Tiffany naked beneath him as he looked down at her. He never allowed women to get to him like this and he was damn sure Tiffany wouldn't be any different. It must be the bizarre situation they were now in. A primal need to claim her as his wife in every way.

He had no time to indulge in such thoughts now. He had a job to do and that was to supply Tiffany with all she would need to carry out her role as his bride-to-be. Whatever else he thought of the state of matrimony and no matter how close he'd come to it once, he had to ensure the woman he'd selected for the role of his bride looked the part, both here and in his kingdom of Shamsumara—the very reason all this was even happening.

'This is Madame Rousseau.' He introduced the world-renowned designer and was pleased to see a moment of surprise on Tiffany's face. 'She will provide you with all you will need for our week in Paris and, of course, your wedding dress.'

Tiffany turned to the older woman and spoke to her in French. 'I am honoured, *madame*.'

Instantly the woman he'd chosen for a bride was winning over the designer and a dart of admiration filled him. It appeared there was much more to Tiffany Chapelle than he'd first thought. Again that need to know more, to find out more, to explore in unchartered waters surfaced.

'You will be the most beautiful bride,' Madame Rousseau praised, obviously pleased to be able to converse in her mother tongue. 'And you will make a fine queen for His Highness.'

Jafar's body stilled. He had not yet explained to Tiffany that her role would entail much more than being his bride, that she would have to assume the role of his Queen for the duration of her stay in Shamsumara.

'She will indeed make a fine queen.' He smiled at her, aware of her scrutiny.

'It's a role I intend to take very seriously,' she said with the biggest smile he'd yet seen on those very kissable lips. Confidence oozed from her, making him sure she could carry it off perfectly and letting him know she accepted the challenge.

'So you have kept your romance secret for the last few months.' Madame Rousseau continued in that wonderfully passionately way she was known for, obviously buying into the story he'd told her. 'How very clever of you both.'

Madame Rousseau instructed with the wave of a pointed finger for Tiffany to turn, and as she did so Tiffany's gaze met his and the sparks of annoyance in her eyes were so powerful and incredibly sexy he had to curtail the need to send the designer away and kiss Tiffany until she begged to be his.

He pushed that urge to one side as he sat waiting while Tiffany was fitted with the first dress, which he'd instructed to be simple but elegant for daytime in Paris, but his mind kept returning to the memory of her last Sunday morning in the short dress with a black leather jacket. Far from expensive, he was sure, but it had made her look a million dollars.

'This one is perfect.'

Madame Rousseau's voice ruptured his thoughts and he looked up to see Tiffany in a black dress, loosely cut yet somehow incredibly sexy. To complete the look she had a black clutch bag and dark sunglasses. The whole look showed off her glorious hair colouring and pale complexion to perfection.

'I agree,' he said, not liking the hard gravelly tone to his voice, and if the expression on Tiffany's face was anything to go by, neither did she. There was that challenge again.

He kept that steely control as Tiffany paraded in many different outfits, some of which he rejected, but most of which he agreed with Madame Rousseau that they would be perfect for her role as his bride-to-be.

'There is one more gown,' Madame Rousseau said. 'The evening dress for the charity event.'

'Charity event?' Tiffany questioned and looked at him, her lovely blue eyes wide, like a captured animal who didn't know whether it should run or stay.

'We have been invited to World Water charity dinner, attended by many famous names.' He had a twinge of guilt as she suddenly looked completely out of her depth. Surely she'd mixed with the rich and famous before as part of her job? She'd certainly sold her business to him as that, which had been one of the main reasons for going through with his plans; he'd been sure she wouldn't be fazed by such occasions.

'Come, come,' the designer said quickly, and Tiffany turned her back on him. He watched her as she walked back into the other room and listened to the delighted sounds from Madame Rousseau.

Even so, he wasn't prepared for the way Tiffany looked as she came into the room again, chin held regally high, her hair quickly pulled up roughly into a chignon. Her pale skin showed the beauty of the black lace, set with black gems, but it was the slit to the top of her thigh he couldn't stop looking at. One pale, slender leg was showcased to perfection as she stood there, taking his appraisal as if she'd been born into the role of a princess to be his Queen. In that moment she was exactly what he wanted in a wife—a real wife. She was desirable and aloof, competent and confident.

What was he doing entertaining such thoughts?

He pushed them roughly aside. 'I agree.' He looked at Madame Rousseau, unsure if he could look into the blue depths of Tiffany's eyes and be able to disguise the powerfully raw desire pounding through him.

Later that evening, after having her hair, nails and make-up professionally done, Tiffany stepped into one of the evening dresses Jafar had selected. Tonight they were to have a romantic dinner at one of the city's top hotels, frequented by rich and famous people from around the world. The bright green fabric of the dress was soft and luxurious against her skin and she couldn't help but admire it, even though she felt like a bought woman.

*That is exactly what you are.* The words taunted her as they played over in her mind. She was Sheikh Jafar Al-Shehri's bought bride.

Jafar's expression as she'd stood waiting for his approval this afternoon had been cold and detached, which only backed up her anxious thoughts. He had been merely approving the items of clothing, ensuring they fitted in with the plans he'd made for the announcement of their engagement.

She looked down at her left hand, where the biggest diamond she'd ever seen glittered on her third finger. It was rose pink and so unusual that, despite the way he'd given it to her after Madame Rousseau had left, as if having it at all was an afterthought, she had been stunned by its beauty.

'You look perfect.' Jafar's voice, the harsh tones of earlier still lingering, dragged her mind back to the present. 'Perfectly beautiful.'

She looked at him, wanting to return the compliment, if that was what it was. His dark suit fitted his tall, athletic body, accentuating his muscular contours that could only come from regular workouts, but as he came closer her words dried on her lips.

'The colour shows your glorious hair off.' He reached out and took the ends of her loose hair between his thumb and fingers and her breath caught audibly in her throat, her gaze meeting the vibrant colour of his. What was this power he had over her? Every nerve cell in her body was on high alert when he was near, waiting for his touch—wanting it.

She should step back, away from his power, but she couldn't. Something dangerous simmered around them but still she couldn't move. Just what was it this man possessed that made her act so differently from normal? Usually she wouldn't entertain anything that was even remotely like flirting. This wasn't flirting. Instinctively she knew this was much deeper, much more primitive, and it excited and scared her at the same time.

'Madame Rousseau's choices are amazing,'

she enthused, desperate to talk of neutral things, needing to calm the erratic thump of her heart.

'I told you,' he practically purred, but she knew this jungle cat was far from docile, 'that when I do something, I do it properly, which is why I always hire Madame Rousseau when I am in Paris.'

'You do?' The question was out before she could stop it. So too was the hurt that she was not the first woman to have been paraded before him like this, kitted out with everything to meet his demanding requirements.

The urge to throw a tantrum, to stamp her foot and march out rushed through her, but the memory of Bethany's face as she'd told her what she was about to do calmed the need to run, the need to be away from this man—as far as possible. It was the hope that had mixed with the shock in her sister's eyes that had convinced her she was doing the right thing and recalling that now would help to keep her focused on what she had to be. A woman of quality that could grace the arm of a man such as Jafar Al-Shehri.

He looked into her eyes and moved closer and

for one heart-stopping moment she thought he was going to kiss her. Properly kiss her. Her lips parted and softened even though panic rushed through her. She did want to be kissed. It wasn't part of their deal but right at that moment she didn't care about the deal or the money. All she cared about was tasting this man on her lips, feeling his breath mix with hers and, most of all, responding in a way she'd never, ever, wanted to do with any man.

Jafar's control had almost slipped. He hadn't even left the hotel suite and all he wanted was to take Tiffany to his bed. Never had a woman had such a profound effect on him, not even his childhood sweetheart, Niesha. But then she had never been forbidden fruit and even if she had her centre would have been poisoned by her greedy ambition, which had showed itself in time to stop him making the biggest mistake of his life and marrying her.

The familiar stab of rage that accompanied thoughts of Niesha was a welcome relief to the hot, searing passion of need coursing through him right now. 'We should go,' he said coldly, swallowing down the taste of betrayal that always reared its head at the thought of just how low Niesha had stooped when she'd married his cousin.

'I think that is best.' The supercilious tone of her voice didn't hide her embarrassment at what had almost happened. There was no denying the blush on her pale skin, which the sexy dusting of freckles couldn't hide.

Had she wanted the kiss? Had she wanted more? He gritted his teeth against the questions, determined to remain in control. All he had to do was remind himself why Tiffany Chapelle was here with him, why she'd agreed to the deal. She was as motivated by money and position as Niesha was. Were all women the same?

The question had hung over him as they dined in the finest restaurant Paris could offer, with views of the Eiffel Tower as it shimmered like gold in the night, then lit up with glimmering lights for the first five minutes of every hour.

He'd thought, having seen it now three times during their meal, that his need, the insatiable desire to kiss Tiffany, would have eased—but it hadn't.

Time to talk business. Maybe that would remind him that she wasn't here for his pleasure, but for the stability of his kingdom. 'When we arrive in Shamsumara there will be a feast. One that is celebrated every year, but this time it will be bigger than normal in honour of your arrival.'

'My arrival? Why?' Had she really thought she could hide herself away from his people?

'You are my bride, Tiffany, and my country has been in a state of upheaval since my brother's death. Your arrival is causing much excitement.'

Her eyes widened in surprise and he fought hard against the urge to smile. Better she thought he was cold and detached.

'Even though I am not from your country?' The doubt and hesitation in her voice were endearing.

'Especially because of that, and also because you will be my Queen.' He sensed her reservations.

'And what is expected of your Queen?' The question darted back at him.

'There will be times when we must be seen together during the three months you are in Shamsumara and that is all I ask of you. To be at my side and show an interest in the kingdom and its people.'

'How can I best do that?'

Her question gave him hope of successfully acting out the marriage in public. 'My aide informs me that you are seen as a new hope and it has been suggested you should build on that, create a project to occupy your time while in Shamsumara. One to call your own.'

He thought of the discussion he'd had with his aide in the days after he and Tiffany had agreed on the deal. He was the only other person who knew that the marriage was a business deal, not just out of the necessity of drawing up the contract, but because he would be best able to serve both Jafar and Tiffany knowing the truth—especially when it came to getting a divorce in two years.

'Like what?' She frowned at him, her lips forming a pout that was so seductive, but with the air of innocence about her right now, he was sure she had no idea just what it did to him.

'There must be a cause which is close to your heart.'

'Well, yes,' she said, suddenly shy, which only enhanced that innocence he found so appealing. 'I'd like to help women who for whatever reason are struggling to bring up children on their own.'

The fact that she didn't have to think about it spoke volumes about the kind of woman she was and he questioned his earlier opinion of her. When he and Niesha had had a similar conversation, many years ago when he'd thought his future would be very different, she'd been unable to instantly come up with anything. That should have been all the warning he needed that she hadn't been suitable princess material, let alone queen, that despite all her so-called suitability she was far from capable of the role.

'A very worthy cause.' He knew it was her sister's plight that had instigated the suggestion, but it made him see her in a different light. She hadn't accepted the deal because it was going to financially benefit her directly. She'd accepted in order to help her sister. 'I shall have my aide put things in motion for you, so that you can take over once the honeymoon is over.'

'I didn't expect us to have a honeymoon.' He watched her swallow, watched the movement of her throat and wanted nothing more than to kiss her there, to feel the softness of her skin.

'It is tradition in my kingdom that a bride and groom spend seven days alone, with only each other for company after the wedding feast.'

'Seven days,' she exclaimed loudly, a little too loudly if the turn of other diners' heads was anything to go by.

'We will be expected to be on our own for the duration of the honeymoon, after which there will be another feast and guests will bring gifts.' He sensed her nerves once again. Why did she not want to be alone with him? Was it because he'd misread the signals, misinterpreted the desire in her eyes? Did she really dislike him?

'It all seems very drawn out. Do we really need to adhere to all that tradition?'

'The tradition comes from the need to ensure the arrival of an heir and as we are taking on the role of lovers wanting to marry, then I am afraid it will have to be observed.'

She sat back, her delicate brows pulled together. 'What about an heir? Will your sister's child really be accepted as your heir?'

She doubted what he'd told her and a flurry of irritation rushed over him. 'I didn't ever want to rule Shamsumara but fate has decreed that I should and I will not let my brother down or turn away from my duty. However, being a father is not something I have ever envisaged for myself and my sister's child will be accepted by the people of my kingdom. I will ensure that.'

'So let me get this straight.' She sat forward, confidence suddenly oozing from her. 'We have to spend seven days locked away, pretending to be newly-wed lovers? How are we going to achieve that?'

Did she not feel the increasing sexual tension between them? Right now he would give anything for her to want him as much as he wanted her. He slammed the idea aside. He could not truly make this woman his wife. If he did, all he'd grown up believing in, the honour and tradition that went with the position of ruler of Shamsumara, would mean that he would be going against it all by divorcing her. He could only do that knowing he'd never consummated the marriage. His beliefs were everything to him.

He was already in turmoil just by going through with the deal with Tiffany but he couldn't stand by and allow Simdan to claim his title, his throne. Just as he couldn't ever drag a woman into the situation of his kingdom by letting her think the marriage meant anything to him. At least Tiffany was well aware of what was expected of her and she'd signed a contract to that effect.

'Our palace quarters will be vast. You will have your own rooms.' He dragged his mind back to the conversation. 'That will ensure the ease of your departure once my sister's baby is born.'

'And what will you tell your people, your officials?' There was accusation in her voice.

'I will state how unhappy you were, how homesick and unsettled. It will be merely a formality.'

'Good,' she replied officiously. 'I have no intention of making this marriage any harder to get out of than it already is.'

'In that case, we understand one another well.'

# CHAPTER FOUR

FOR THE LAST six days Tiffany had tried to avoid being with Jafar as much as possible, which had been far easier than she'd ever imagined, as he too seemed to have had the same idea, especially when they were alone. If they had been together, it was in public, and when they were in the suite it was so big she could easily hide herself away. It was also exactly how she hoped it would be once they were in Shamsumara and not at all like her recent dreams, which had been full of images of Jafar in the desert, white robes blowing in the warm wind. He was fast becoming her fantasy and that was the last thing she wanted or needed right now.

To counteract these sensual dreams, during the day, when she had been on her own, she'd thought back to his almost callous use of his sister and her child. The fact that he'd calmly told her his sister's child would be his heir made her view him in a different light. He was powerful and more than prepared to exert that power to get what he wanted. No matter how outrageously sexy he had been in her dreams, by day he was the epitome of all she hated in a man—just wrapped up in a very sexy package. And it was this sexy packaging that was causing her the most concern. She'd never been so affected by a man before. She felt trapped in a web of desire she had no idea how to escape from and was totally unprepared for how to deal with a man like the Sheikh of Shamsumara.

On her finger was the biggest diamond she'd ever seen and in her mind Bethany's words of shock continued to play.

*'He is hiring you as his bride? Why are you agreeing to it? Why are you going off to some far-flung country? Please don't do it—not for us.'*

Tiffany had remained firm, knowing that there was no other way she or Bethany could ever find enough money to keep a roof over their heads. It wasn't just for Bethany and her daughter now, it was for herself too after she'd given up renting her apartment and moved in with her sister to help out with loan payments. It had been enough to keep the wolf from howling at the door, but it wouldn't last long. Jafar's offer had come at the right time and there was no way she was going to let it pass.

With a sigh of regret for all that had happened over the last few years she looked out over the city of Paris, the glow of yellow lights giving it a surreal feel. It was the most perfect place and she'd longed to visit it for many years, but if someone had told her she would be here engaged to a desert sheikh, about to become his wife as part of a deal, she would have said they were crazy.

*'He is hiring you as his bride?'*

Again Bethany's words careered into all other thoughts and she took a deep breath, trying to compose herself. She was dressed in the most exquisite black lace dress and she felt like a princess on the outside. But inside she was a complete mess.

'The city is beautiful tonight, is it not?' Jafar's voice paused the words in her mind as they looped again and again. She turned to look at him, instantly wishing she hadn't.

He was dressed in his usual suit, but there was something different about him. He looked powerful and commanding and devastatingly handsome. The black suit over a pastel lavender shirt made him appear much taller, much more powerful. Or was it her nerves that did that?

'I wish I could be up there,' she said as she looked towards the Eiffel Tower, lit up in the darkness. 'Paris is so lovely I don't want to leave.'

She had expected him to brush off her comment with yet another of his harsh comments. They'd been coming thick and fast all week and she was seriously wondering how she would be able to spend another week ensconced with him after their marriage. The sooner that part of their deal was over, the better.

'If it makes you feel any better, neither do I.'

She looked up at him, into his handsome face, and into eyes that seemed full of emotions she couldn't read. 'I appreciate this week has been tough, but you have proved many times over you are more than capable of being my Queen. I have no doubt you will be perfect, but if you do want to back out, now is the time—the last chance you will have.'

'I'm not going to back out.' She forgot the amazing view, the romance of a city she longed to explore better, rising to the challenge he was most certainly throwing her way. 'Whatever else you think of me, Jafar, I honour my promise.'

'That is all I need to know,' he said as if gentling a startled animal. 'Because once we arrive in Shamsumara tomorrow there will be no going back.'

He moved towards her and the warm evening air became charged with that same spark she'd tried to ignore on their first night in Paris. The night when she had been fool enough to think he might actually kiss her. He had spoken softly then too, lured her into a false sense of security, bringing down almost all her barriers even if only for the briefest time.

'Don't we have to be somewhere?' She moved quickly past him and into the room, away from the romance of the view, the balcony, the open window with lace rippling in the breeze.

'We do indeed.' The words had hardened. The Jafar she'd come to know over the last week was back. A man in control, a man for whom sentiments were not something he indulged in. So who was the man who had just slipped to the surface? Which was the real Jafar?

'I'd like to go, get it over with.' He frowned at her comment. 'Arriving in front of the press, that is. It might be normal for you, but I have not experienced such a thing, not when the attention is thrown at me.'

Jafar had never seen such a pack of photographers, all vying for the best shot. Tiffany had been right to worry. The car stopped outside the hotel entrance where a red carpet led the guests into the World Water charity dinner he attended most years, but news of their engagement was spreading fast and now the press were ferociously hungry for a story.

He should have known better. His playboy reputation, together with his wealth and now the speculation as to what would happen to his country after his brother's death, was not just creating interest in his own kingdom, but worldwide. It was sure to become worse now that his chosen bride had been revealed, mostly due to the fact that she was English. Now more than ever it was important to show a façade of lovers eager to be married.

Beside him he sensed Tiffany tense, sensed not only her reservations, but fear. Again he wondered why, when she'd told him her work brought her into contact with the rich and famous. Surely she'd been in the thick of something like this before as a bridesmaid. She must at least be used to media attention.

He took her hand, momentarily taken aback by the smallness of hers as he turned to face the press who looked more like baying wolves. 'Just be yourself.' He moved closer to her and spoke softly in her ear but in doing so inhaled the scent of bergamot and rosewood. It made him think of home as yet more Eastern scents invaded his senses. Was this her usual perfume or had she changed to one he would recognise and react to? Was it to tempt him, to lay down another challenge?

'So who will be your bridesmaid?' one of the photographers shouted as she lifted her chin and smiled at the cameras, again making him think that, whatever else she was, she was born to the role he'd created for her for the next three months. She could easily put on the show of confidence even though he could sense her reservations, her fear.

'All will be revealed very soon, gentlemen.' This was a discussion he needed to have with her this evening. He had his own plans, which he'd put in motion as part of a thank-you gesture to her, but he still needed to ensure she was happy with the idea.

He looked down as she glanced up at him,

surprise in the depths of her eyes. In that moment he knew he would do all he could to ensure that her sister and niece filled those roles as he'd planned. That spark of fire he'd felt the first night in Paris shot through him once more and as her lips parted he couldn't help himself. He had to kiss her.

The noise of everything else subsided into nothingness as he lowered his head and, meeting no resistance from her, he brushed his lips over hers, testing and teasing. What he hadn't expected was the sigh of pleasure from her, or for her to move her lips against his, to respond and demand. What was she trying to do to him? Just when he thought he might lose his mind, his control and his ability to think, camera flashes popped all around him, bringing him startlingly back to reality and he pulled away from her, but didn't miss the confusion in her eyes.

She had been playing out the role he'd instructed her to. Why else would she have spent all week avoiding being with him unless they were out in company and then kiss him like that?

'Finally the bride,' another photographer taunted.

'Not the bridesmaid this time,' one said in heavily accented English, making it clear they knew all about her.

He was sure Tiffany shrank back a little, making him want to ram the camera down the man's throat. The need to protect this woman was fierce and distinctly primal. It was also one he'd never experienced before.

'That's enough,' he growled as he turned and led Tiffany into the hotel. 'Damn pack of wolves.'

'I had no idea it was so intense being the centre of their attention,' she said as they moved into the sanctuary of the hotel lobby. 'And you just made it worse when you kissed me.'

The censure in her voice was clear and the image she created, standing against the backdrop of luxury within the hotel, was overwhelmingly beautiful and he found himself thinking how stunning she would look dressed in the Eastern wardrobe he'd had prepared for her arrival at his palace.

'Only to ensure there is no doubt about our relationship.' Who was he trying to fool? It was simply because he'd wanted to, had been unable to resist the temptation those soft, full, lipstick-covered lips had presented. 'And you played your part admirably.'

'Just like you, Jafar, when I do something I do it properly.' His earlier words came back at him like a bolt of lightning.

'Then may I suggest you take my arm and accompany me into the charity dinner where we can both play our parts to perfection?'

The next few hours passed slowly and all he could think about was the woman sitting next to him and the brief but powerful kiss they'd shared. Because they had shared it. She had kissed him back, had wanted it to go on, to become something else as much as he had. Whatever it was between them it was mutual—just as the resistance was.

Each time he looked at her, the elegance of the black lace dress begged him to remove it, begged him to reveal all that pale skin. What would it look like next to the darkness of his? Erotic images surged forward like a tidal wave and he pressed his thumb and one finger on each temple, his hand covering his eyes. What the hell was wrong with him? Maybe he should just kiss her and get it out of his system?

No, one kiss would unleash more need, more fire and desire. He was in no doubt of that.

'Let's go,' he said as the speeches finished, not caring what their early departure would look like. He just wanted her for himself.

'Where are we going now?'

As she become embroiled in goodbyes with those at their table, he took the opportunity and made the call to put in motion a plan to spend time with just Tiffany, to indulge her in the one thing she wanted to do in Paris but hadn't been able to. *It's just a token of thanks*, he told himself, but deep down knew it was much more, just as flying her sister and niece to the wedding was. He wanted to make her happy.

'To the restaurant in the tower,' he said, sliding his phone back into his inside pocket.

'But we've eaten.' The alarm in her voice made him smile.

'I want to show you Paris, take you to the one place you said you wanted to visit, as a thank-you. Once we are in my homeland we will be busy with feasts and celebrations. Tonight will be for us.'

She looked at him with big eyes, making her appear vulnerable and sexy at the same time, and for a moment he thought he was drowning and that she was the only woman who could save him.

'I'd like that.' Her breathy whisper sent the spark of lust throbbing through him afresh and he was thankful his car had arrived.

Tiffany wanted to look away from the intensity in his eyes but she couldn't. He might not be physically close to her but the overpowering pull of attraction between them was becoming harder to ignore—and much more difficult to resist.

'So would I.' Jafar's voice was deep and husky, his unmistakable accent more pronounced, and it sent shivers of awareness down her spine. When he took her hand and led her to the waiting car she almost pulled back, the fire of his touch so hot.

Was this too just an act, like that intense yet very light kiss he'd brushed over her lips earlier? Was he continuing the act of lovers in the grip of a whirlwind romance? She pushed the questions away, refusing to think too much, only knowing that she intended to enjoy this night, make the most of the romance that was unexpectedly lingering in the air—real or not. Lilly's suggestion that she have a fling to get over her ex came to the fore. Could Jafar be that man to help her heal her wounds? Maybe it was just being in Paris, the city for lovers, but right now she wanted him to be exactly that.

Jafar's car negotiated the busy Parisian traffic and Tiffany focused her attention on the tower as they approached it—anything other than look at the man beside her. The air inside the car sparked with something so unfamiliar that her heart pounded. At last the car stopped and within minutes she and Jafar were inside the elevator on their way up to the restaurant. Except that was worse than the car—far more confined. This time she focused on watching the iconic gold-coloured metal structure of the tower as they went higher, praying that it wouldn't be much longer before they were at the restaurant.

'I thought it would be busier.' Her words trailed off in wonder as they stepped out of the elevator. She looked around the restaurant and beyond the wall of windows to the city of Paris. It was breathtakingly beautiful.

'The final service of the evening is almost over, but they have agreed to cater to our special occasion and I have arranged for a table with the best view.' The command in his voice was clear and the implications that he could just arrange whatever he pleased wasn't lost on her.

'I didn't expect this,' she said and fixed her attention on the view because she couldn't look at him, not when she could still feel the heat of his lips on hers.

As they were seated at the table with an unrivalled view of the Palais de Chaillot, Tiffany could feel herself falling under the spell of romance. She fought it, but it was all too much to resist, the soft music playing in the background, the view, but most of all the man himself.

'I need to know who you would like to attend the wedding.' Jafar dropped the question between them, shattering the illusion of romance she'd allowed to build up inside her. 'What about your sister and your niece to be your bridesmaids?'

Was this an afterthought because of what the reporters had asked as they'd arrived? Did he see their attendance as a way of validating the marriage, making it appear more real? 'Do we really need to involve them? It's not as if the marriage is for real.'

'I thought you would welcome a friendly face.'

'Or give the whole thing the appearance of being more real.' She couldn't keep the hurt from her voice, but at least that stab of pain was more preferable than the soft, romantic notions it had just replaced. 'Do whatever you want. I doubt Bethany will come anyway.'

After the way her sister had pleaded with her not to go through with the marriage, that they would find another way to sort out the financial mess they were in, she doubted Bethany would have anything to do with the actual marriage ceremony—especially if it meant travelling to another country. There was no way she could afford a plane ticket anywhere right now.

'What about your best friend?' His question surprised her and she tried to think if she'd spoken to him of Lilly.

'How do you know about Lilly?'

'I don't.' There was a hint of amusement in his voice and it confused her. She was trying to be irritated with him and all these questions were just pushing her back to the notion that he cared, that there was an undercurrent of something romantic between them. 'I just know every woman has one.'

'I haven't told Lilly yet.' She knew full well that Lilly knew after the texts she'd received this last week. Bethany must have told her and she owed her friend a call to explain just what it was she was doing and why. All she needed was the confidence to actually tell her with conviction.

'I'd like your parents to be there too. I want to make sure you feel comfortable on your wedding day, Tiffany—and happy.' His voice had softened, as if he really did care, and she recalled the shock on her mother's and father's faces as she'd told them she was in love and getting married. She hadn't been able to tell either of them the truth.

'You are making a good show of it.' She threw the hot words back at him, needing to cover up the flutter of attraction that was threatening once more to erupt and overflow.

He took her hand across the table. She should pull back, shouldn't look into his eyes, but she couldn't do anything she thought she should do. She was once again well and truly under his spell.

'Nothing about tonight has been for show.' There was fierceness to his words, as if he too was fighting the growing attraction between them. The fact that he wanted her, found her attractive, only heightened hers for him. She wanted to be desired by him—and so much more.

'But we agreed nothing would happen between us.' Her voice was a whisper and there was a glint of satisfaction in his eyes. Had she walked into a trap of her own making? Right now she didn't care. She wanted to be caught by this man.

'We can also agree to enjoy this moment for what it is.' His thumb and finger were caressing her hand, making thought impossible.

Her breath hitched noticeably. 'What is this moment, Jafar?'

'The moment when a man and woman who are attracted to one another forget all else and live just for the moment.' His poetic words sealed her fate and she was eternally grateful they were in a restaurant where nothing other than holding hands across the table could happen.

He let her hand go and stood up, towering over her and the table, dominating every bit of space, every bit of air she breathed. 'Let us make the most of the impressive view.'

'But what of other diners?'

'They have all gone.' That self-assured satisfaction was back in his voice. 'As have the staff.'

'We are alone?'

'Alone enough to enjoy the romantic view, yes. I have paid well for this and want to share this moment in Paris with you.'

He held out his hand for her and she took it, placed her napkin on the table and stood up, but as he didn't move it brought her very close to him. Close enough to kiss him if she had the courage.

She lowered her chin, averted her eyes from that powerful gaze, but with his free hand he lifted her chin back up, forced her to look into his eyes. His sparked with gold as they bored into her soul, dragging her from her corner of self-doubt.

'I want to kiss you, Tiffany.'

Now she couldn't move, couldn't look away. He'd successfully snared her, catching her in his trap, and all she wanted was release. The kind of release that would only come from feeling his lips on hers, not for show because cameras were flashing, but for real.

'I want that too. I want you to kiss me,' she whispered, her heart thumping so hard it sounded in her head like a drum.

He moved his fingers from her chin and stroked the side of his thumb over her cheek and her eyelashes fluttered and closed at the sensation of fire and heat that bubbled up from deep within her. She shouldn't be doing this at all, but everything felt so right, so real, how could she not?

'You are so beautiful.' His hoarse whisper only stoked that fire higher and she opened her eyes. He moved closer, his hand sliding round to the back of her head, holding her right where he wanted her.

Her breath was deep and hard and she knew her breasts were rising and falling rapidly as desire began to consume her. She parted her lips as he moved closer still, his eyes locked on hers. Should she close hers, block out the image of his swirling with hot passion?

His lips touched hers and she closed her eyes, pulling herself against him, snagging in a breath as her body made contact with his. He pulled her hard against him with his free arm. She could feel the muscled contours of his chest, the strength in his arm and, more potently, the hardness of his arousal as her body responded, moulding her to him in a way that set loose the fire of desire she'd been hoping to control.

He murmured something against her lips and she sank deeper into the desire that was now flooding through her. The kiss hardened, became more demanding, but instead of pulling back, instead of ending it as she knew she should do, she returned the kiss with a fever she'd never thought possible. His hand gripped her harder at the back of her neck, angling her head so that he could force her lips apart and plunder her mouth with his tongue. She gasped her pleasure into his mouth, which only made him demand more from her.

Then as suddenly as it all started he stopped, let her go and she staggered backwards, gasping for breath as she clutched at the back of the chair. His desire-heavy gaze travelled down her body as if he were physically removing the black lace dress from her and, although it was so wrong, right now it was precisely what she wanted him to do.

'Perhaps we should return to our suite.' The firmness of his voice shocked her. Didn't he feel the same wild passion thumping through him? 'To sleep alone, as the tradition of my country dictates.'

'I think in light of our deal that is the best thing to do.' Inside she was crying out for him, wanting his kiss and more. Thankfully her head was once more ruling the situation, crushing down the passion he'd evoked with that kiss, the like of which she'd never before experienced. She'd only ever kissed her previous boyfriend and that had always been a chaste affair, but what she'd just shared with Jafar had been dangerous yet wildly exciting.

'As you wish.' He turned from her and she knew the moment was gone, that they were back on track, back to being two people entering a business deal. The lovers that had surfaced briefly were well and truly suppressed.

## CHAPTER FIVE

THE SEARING INTENSITY of the kiss last night in Paris soon became overshadowed by the reality of being in the desert kingdom of Shamsumara, where Jafar was obviously respected by his people. Tiffany had a twinge of guilt for deceiving them, but determinedly she pushed it aside. The fake marriage had never been her idea and, yes, she would be benefitting, but it was all about Jafar getting what he wanted, preventing his cousin from claiming the kingdom as his own. Would she meet this cousin now she was here?

The palace was beautifully striking and the early evening sun was casting a gold glow over all the intricately decorated archways they were walking through. She followed her husband-to-be, his long purposeful strides hard to keep up with as she tried to look around her too.

This would be her home for the next three months. Jafar paused outside a set of ornate doors. The thought hit her that tomorrow he would be her husband and for the next three months they would be expected to live together as man and wife. She thought again of the kiss in Paris. Could she be with him for that time and not want to be kissed again?

'This will be our suite, but for this evening I will be at the opposite end of the palace as tradition dictates.' The velvety tones of his voice were still evident despite the authority in his words and relief rushed through her; she was thankful that she wouldn't have to spend time alone with him tonight when all she could think about was last night. Her body still ached for him, her lips desperate to feel his claiming hers once more.

Last night had been a reckless mistake and she couldn't allow it to happen again.

'Of course, I wouldn't have expected anything less.' She walked into the room, stunned at the height of the ceilings. Through an archway that was almost key-shaped she could see a bed draped in gold silks and much bigger than any she'd ever seen. Gold lace hung from a frame above the bed and rested behind the array of pillows and cushions. It was opulent, luxurious and totally beyond anything she could have imagined.

It also signified exactly what their marriage was to be about as far as his kingdom was concerned. Tiffany was shocked at the regret that fluttered after that thought. She wanted to be in that bed, with Jafar. She wanted to explore what it was her body was begging for whenever he was close.

'The bridal bed,' Jafar said, coming to stand directly behind her, and she blushed at her wayward thoughts. He lowered his voice to a whisper, making her breath catch, her body heat. 'We will be expected to share it tomorrow night. Or at least make it appear as if we are, but for this evening you can enjoy it alone.'

'It's quite beautiful and the perfect place for a desert king and his bride to be ensconced for a week—if it were all for real.' She had to set some boundaries for herself as much as him, because if she didn't she was sure she would want to be kissed like last night again and she had to remember this wasn't a real marriage. This was a deal. He'd paid her and paid her well. Whatever else was between them, it meant nothing.

'Don't be fooled that this isn't for real, Tiffany. This time tomorrow you *will* be my wife.'

She turned to face him and instantly wished she hadn't. His eyes darkened, becoming like the depths of the forest where the sun didn't reach even at the height of the day. 'The ceremony will be real, as will the three months I am to remain here, but nothing else. Our *marriage* is a deal, nothing more.'

How was she going to spend a whole week in his company, in a setting as blissfully romantic as this, and not want him to kiss her—or more? Last night she'd tasted the kind of paradise she'd thought only existed in dreams, the kind of passion and desire she'd never thought herself capable of. She should never have given into the need her body had suddenly craved. A need only this man could meet. She was losing control fast and needed to find it again if she stood any chance of making it through the next week, let alone the next three months.

'We understand one another well, I think,' he said as several women slipped in through the open door behind them. 'Now that your maids have arrived to be your chaperones, I will leave you in their capable hands and you can be assured that you will not have to be alone with me at all until after tomorrow's celebrations.'

Tiffany watched him go, aware of the speculation of the young women watching her. Would they speak English? How was she going to manage without Jafar to guide her? The urge to call him back almost made her rush from the room; instead she pulled off the black headscarf she'd been instructed to wear for their arrival. She was in the company of only women now and could relax—a little at least.

'Your hair is so beautiful.' One of the maids stepped forward with a friendly smile, making Tiffany suddenly shy and so pleased too that she could at least talk to someone in English. 'My name is Aaleyah and we are here to serve you. A bath is drawn and your clothes for the feast this evening are ready.'

Relief filled Tiffany as she instantly sensed she might have an ally in Aaleyah. 'I'd like to ensure I do things right,' she said, hoping to instil authority into her voice instead of the nerves fluttering through her. 'I hope that you will help me.'

'Of course,' Aaleyah said, her English very good. 'That is what we are here for.'

Jafar had been anxious for Tiffany as he'd walked away from the Royal Suite. He was glad now he'd put in motion the idea of her sister, friend and parents attending the wedding tomorrow before he'd even mentioned it to her. It would be a fitting surprise for her and at least she would have familiar faces around her. It was no different from what he would have done if they had been embarking on a real marriage.

The idea of a real marriage with Tiffany, of truly making her his wife, sent a rush of throbbing lust through him. If this were a real marriage, then tomorrow night they would be together in the bridal bed, exploring the passion that sparked between them. Passion he knew she felt too, despite her words of bravado.

Now he waited for her arrival at the feast. Her first public appearance. When she finally arrived, nerves were clearly etched onto her beautiful face but as she entered the banqueting hall, her entourage of women following closely, he let a breath of relief escape him. She looked absolutely stunning and completely regal.

Beneath the black silk *abaya*, which she wore open, he could see her silver dress, fitting her sensually curvy body yet conforming to the traditions expected of his bride-to-be on the feast before their wedding. Her lovely deep brown hair was piled up on her head, which was covered in fine black chiffon. He imagined removing the chiffon and unpinning her hair, letting it tumble down her back.

He'd seriously have to get better control of his libido before tomorrow evening. He had no intention of making the marriage a true marriage by consummating it and his aide's words of caution came back to him like a spirit on the desert wind.

*'You will have no choice, sire, but to remain married to your English bride for two years. Your ability to rule will be brought into question if the marriage is not seen to be real—just as it will if you are not seen to be spending the first week of marriage alone with your bride.'*

The only thing in jeopardy if he gave into the building desire for the woman he'd hired as his bride was his honour—and honour was everything to him.

He focused his mind elsewhere. There was nothing he wanted less than any questions over his claim as the rightful ruler of Shamsumara. If it hadn't been for his cousin's underhand attempts at taking over the kingdom after his brother's death, he would never have had to find a bride and do the one thing he really didn't want to do.

Tiffany took her place at his side as he sat on the raised platform at the top of the banqueting hall. She settled onto the large red and gold cushions, not at all fazed by how unfamiliar such an arrangement must be to her, and it struck him that she too was as calculated in accepting his offer as Niesha, the woman he'd always believed would one day be his wife, had been.

'How was your evening?' He was well aware that she would have been bathed in scented water and then pampered before being helped into her dress and tomorrow it would be even more of a ritual. Tomorrow she would be being prepared for him—his pleasure. He shoved the thought aside, angry at his lack of control yet again as his body heated at the thought of holding her again, kissing. Was it so wrong to desire the woman you were about to marry, even if only for convenience?

'A little daunting. I am beginning to wonder why I'm here, if I can do it,' she confessed and he didn't miss the fact that she wouldn't look him in the eye. Was it because she was trying to be sensitive to his kingdom's culture or because she trusted herself as little as he did? Part of him hoped it was the latter.

'It's too late for that now.' His fierce tone was

born out of the need to be totally in control, something which, if he was honest, he'd barely been around this woman. Especially last night. Memories of the kiss, of her lips against his for a second time, obliterated the tenuous grip on his control. It was a kiss that had felt very real, not at all like the staged one as they'd arrived at the charity event.

'I have no intention of backing out. I need the money. Remember?'

As if he needed reminding of the terms of their deal—his marriage. Irritated by her aloofness, even though it was probably for the best, he turned his attention to the newly arrived guests.

His cousin Simdan's perfectly timed arrival, just after Tiffany, only highlighted how much of a threat this man was to Shamsumara. He was as threatening to the success of what he and Tiffany were doing as his wife, Niesha, and their young son were. She was the woman he himself should have married if her need to do better than the spare heir of Shamsumara, as he was then, hadn't forced her to break their long-standing engagement and marry Simdan. He had grown up knowing he was to marry Niesha, but Simdan was more than welcome to such a scheming woman. Whatever his cousin thought, Jafar was adamant that Simdan wasn't going to take his kingdom with the same ease he'd taken his promised bride—or at all.

'Good, because my cousin and his wife have just arrived. As the closest members of my family other than my sister, they will be joining us here.'

'The cousin who is threatening to take over your country?' She looked at him now that the attention was not directly on them or the simmering sexual tension that was threatening to explode in the most spectacular fashion. Disbelief filled her eyes.

'The very same.' He just had time to confirm her question before Simdan sat beside him. He spoke in his own language, the undertone of warning to his cousin clear whatever any bystander understood and he was aware of Niesha's cold, curious gaze on Tiffany. How could he ever have thought he could come to love Niesha, to want to spend the rest of his life with such a woman at his side? She was as wrong for him as Tiffany was.

'Simdan, Niesha, may I introduce my bride, Tiffany?' He spoke in English as knowing that Niesha understood the language made saying those words all the more satisfying. His cousin's eyes narrowed and he glared hostilely at Tiffany, but it was Niesha's angry eyes that rang alarm bells in his head. She had married his cousin and that fact alone made her capable of just about anything. Would she pose a threat to Tiffany or was he allowing irrational thoughts to get the better of him?

'I am honoured to be joining your bridal entourage,' Niesha said silkily, and already he was having misgivings about allowing the traditions of extended female family members attending the bride. He should have insisted Niesha couldn't be part of that, but had been wary of alerting his cousin to anything that might lead him to the fact that the marriage was merely a deal brokered in an English hotel garden with a woman who made a living out of being a professional bridesmaid.

'I'd be grateful for your guidance,' Tiffany said firmly and he had the distinct impression that she had already assessed Niesha.

'It is time we men withdrew.' He looked at Tiffany and again that sensation that he was abandoning her came over him. 'Your ladies will take care of you and tomorrow, when I see you, it will be to become your husband.'

Tiffany looked up into his eyes as he took her hand and helped her to stand. The warmth of Jafar's touch sent a tingle of awareness all through her, swiftly followed by the realisation that tomorrow her life would change. It didn't matter that the marriage wasn't for love and that they would lead separate lives in three months, tomorrow still changed everything—for her and for Bethany.

'And is everything in place for all my requests to be met?' She kept her voice low, aware that some members of their party spoke very good

English, but also needed to refer to their deal. It was the only thing that would serve as a much-needed reminder for her that this was a business deal, one that would gain each of them what they needed. It would be all too easy to slip into the fake world of affection and, even more so, the illusion of desire. Except, for her, that desire was very real. It was powerful and threatened to consume her. 'Do I have all I asked for?'

His jaw clenched and his lips drew into a severe line. He looked formidable, his eyes sparking a warning at her as he let go of her hand. 'Everything is as planned.'

She wished now she'd insisted on Bethany being with her tomorrow. She wanted reassurance from her sister that he'd kept his part of the deal, because there was no way she was going to tie herself in the legal bindings of marriage to a man who upset her equilibrium so completely she lost all sense of reason unless the money had been transferred. She had to keep the money at the forefront of her mind. Remind herself why she was here.

'Good.' The word sounded cold and officious and from the quick rise of his brows he'd noticed it too. 'So I can call Bethany tomorrow and tell her everything is sorted?'

'She knows the full details of our arrangement?' His voice lowered and his eyes narrowed in suspicion, then he looked around them, checking to see who was paying them any attention.

'Only Bethany. I had to tell her something.' A sense of triumph sluiced over her. In this one thing at least she had some power.

'Make sure it stays that way.' The deep, almost feral growl of his voice dragged her attention back to him and she smiled sweetly, uneasy as she became aware of Niesha watching them closely. She wasn't a fool. She hadn't missed the undercurrent of tension between the man she was to marry and the beautiful Niesha.

'I do things properly,' she quoted his words back at him once more and got the same satisfaction as last time.

'Sorry to break you two up.' Niesha's words cut through the air like a knife and she saw Jafar inhale deeply. 'It's time for the ladies to go. There is much preparation still to do for tomorrow.'

Tiffany looked at Jafar, seeking some sort of guidance or reassurance, the thought of being abandoned to this woman again unsettling. Was Tiffany overreacting to feel threatened by her, by something between her and Jafar?

'There is one more thing.' Jafar pointedly ignored Niesha's intrusion. 'I have arranged a surprise for you, which should by now be waiting in your suite.'

'A surprise?'

'Isn't a man allowed to give gifts to the woman he is to marry?' There was jest in his voice, but Tiffany had the distinct impression it was for Niesha's benefit, all part of the act of a couple madly in love. Maybe there wasn't even a surprise at all.

'Thank you,' she said softly, wanting only to escape the undercurrent of attraction that still sizzled between her and Jafar.

'Then I bid you goodnight.' He looked into her eyes as if he was sending her a special message—but what? 'I will be waiting for you tomorrow.'

Tiffany entered her suite, Jafar's last words ringing in her mind. Niesha and one other lady followed her in, apparently to be her chaperones for the night. She was tired from travelling and fighting the deepening attraction for the man she would marry tomorrow and didn't feel in the mood for any kind of surprise.

'Tiffany. You look amazing. Different, but amazing.' At the sound of her sister's voice she whirled round to see, not only Bethany, but her niece, Kelly, looking so excited to be part of the surprise Jafar had arranged to be waiting here for her. He'd done this for her? Her heart softened a bit more towards the formidable desert sheikh who'd bought the next two years of her life.

'Oh, my goodness. When did you get here?' She rushed over and scooped up Kelly, whirling the little girl around and then stopping to look at her as she held her in her arms.

'You look like a princess.' Kelly's voice was full of awe.

'She is a princess now.' Bethany moved towards them and together they all hugged one another. Then she stepped back. 'There is one more surprise.'

Tiffany looked at her sister, unable to fathom out what that could be. 'What can be better than my two most favourite people in the world?'

'Your best friend?' Lilly's voice sounded from behind and she turned, still holding Kelly, to look at her friend, guilt rushing over her for not having responded to her texts.

'I had to come and see for myself if you really wanted to go through with this and why.' Lilly moved to join them, a teasing smile on her face. 'Of course, I know the supposed real reason, but have also realised there is another very valid reason.'

'There is?' Tiffany was stunned. What other reason could there be other than to help Bethany and Kelly?

'Your groom.' Lilly looked at Kelly, appearing to search for suitable words. 'He is very handsome, not to mention caring for his bride. He arranged all this. He flew us here in secret, as a surprise for you. That tells me a lot—as does your blush.'

'I am not blushing,' Tiffany said quickly, knowing full well she was doing exactly that.

'I think I will put Kelly to bed now.' Bethany touched Tiffany's arm and smiled. 'You two must have lots to catch up on.'

'Before you go…' She halted, not sure how to ask. 'Have all the funds been paid in?'

Bethany looked at her, relief in her eyes. 'Yes.' The word was a whisper and then she silently turned and walked away with a tired Kelly in her arms.

Tiffany watched her sister go, smiling as Kelly waved at her over her shoulder, and she knew that, whatever else Lilly was reading into her motives for accepting this deal with Jafar, she'd done the right thing. Already there was lightness in Bethany's step, a hint of hope in her eyes. Jafar had kept his part of their deal and now she had to keep hers.

'As you have your sister and friend here now, we will leave you and return in the morning to begin the bridal preparations.' Niesha slipped from the shadows of the room, startling Tiffany. She'd completely forgotten about them. Had Niesha just heard that exchange?

'Yes, thank you.' She managed to project calmness as she spoke but didn't miss the look on Niesha's face and wondered again just what it was that had been—or even was—between her and Jafar.

As the two Shamsumarian women left the suite Tiffany looked at Lilly. It was time for the difficult explanation she'd been avoiding.

'Right, Miss Arabian Princess.' Lilly took her arm and propelled her to the living area of the suite, which had looked out over the sculpted sand dunes during the day, but now showcased a velvety blackness full of sparkling stars. 'I need to know everything that is going on and I mean everything.'

After Tiffany had relayed the story, from the moment at the last wedding when she was a bridesmaid for his friend Damian Cole, to the moment at the charity dinner in Paris, she sat back and looked at her friend.

'So let me get this straight.' Lilly's expression of disbelief echoed all she felt as she'd told her almost everything that had happened in the last two weeks. 'He kissed you, in front of the cameras as part of the deal, and you can honestly say you felt nothing?'

Tiffany sighed. 'No and that's the problem.'

'No, it's not. The problem is that you won't let go, can't allow yourself a bit of fun. This could be the perfect opportunity to bury the past, have a fling, prove you don't need your dream of happy ever afters to enjoy yourself.'

'I don't call a two-year marriage contract enjoying myself.' Tiffany bounced out of the chair and began to pace the room, pausing to look out of the window at the beauty of the night.

'Are you kidding?' Lilly said from behind her. 'It's the perfect excuse and Jafar is exactly the right man to fool around with, have some fun, forget about your ex and live a little.'

'I'm not sure.' Tiffany turned and looked at

Lilly unable to hide the truth much longer, and that wasn't the truth about her lack of sexual experience that even Lilly didn't know, but the truth about her deepening feelings and strengthening attraction for Jafar.

'You're blushing,' Lilly said as she rushed over to her, grasping her arms and looking into her face. 'You like him, don't you? A lot?'

'If he kissed me like he did after the party I don't think I could resist him.'

'Hold up. *After* the party?'

Tiffany recounted the kiss that had unlocked all the emotions she'd been trying to hide as well as opening the door for the woman she wanted to be, enabling her to set herself free if she just took the chance.

'Tomorrow night is your wedding night,' Lilly said, looking at her earnestly. 'You are going to be married to him for two years whatever happens, so make the most of it—and the week you have to shut yourself away from the world, which, by the way, I'd gladly do with him.'

To make the most of the week with Jafar, to

enjoy his company, to explore the attraction, was what Tiffany wanted more than anything else. She was falling for Jafar, falling for a man who'd struck a deal with her, bought her for a huge sum of money, but none of that mattered when he looked at her with dark desire in his eyes.

Tomorrow she would be his wife and shockingly, she finally admitted to herself, she wanted to be his wife in the truest sense of the word. 'I told him it was to be a marriage in name only.'

'He's a hot-blooded male, Tiff, and you are an attractive woman.'

'I'm his bought bride. Hired to do the job.' Tiffany tried to talk reason into herself as much as her friend. The admission that she wanted Jafar, wanted to be his wife in every sense, suddenly changed everything for her. After all the resistance she'd put up, could she really change the goalposts now?

# CHAPTER SIX

THE BRIDAL PREPARATION Niesha had referred to last night at the feast had been far more intensive than anything Tiffany had encountered before. She'd seen brides pampered but never to the extent that she had been in the last twelve hours. Now she stood in her white gown, encrusted with an intricate pattern of the tiniest diamonds down the front of the full skirt, and on the fitted bodice they were set against what she suspected was real gold. A sense of panic rushed over her as at any moment the tall doors of the palace banqueting hall would be opened and she would walk towards the man she was to marry.

Nerves raced through her. Could she really do this?

*You are doing it for Bethany.*

Her ladies fussed around her one last time, adjusting the white veil clipped in her hair, which had been scented and elaborately piled on top of her head. Her full skirt was arranged around her one last time. There wasn't a detail they missed, even checking the gold and diamond band at her waist, which showed off her figure while maintaining the modesty of being covered as tradition dictated.

*And you are doing this for Kelly.*

She looked at her niece as she and Bethany were treated to the same attention. She smiled at Kelly, who was having a wonderful time being a little princess. The little girl's laughter made her smile and chased away the doubts that had been building since the moment she'd opened her eyes early this morning. As did Bethany's carefree smile.

Tiffany's attention fell on Lilly, who was less than enamoured with the long-sleeved bridesmaid dresses Madame Rousseau had arranged. The very fact that there were bridesmaids' dresses prepared for them by the designer meant Jafar must have planned from the day they agreed on their deal to have Lilly, Bethany and Kelly at the wedding, as her bridesmaids.

He had mentioned her parents on that night in Paris and she wondered how he'd fared with her mother and father, who hadn't spoken to one another for many years. Jafar was a man who relished a challenge so she wouldn't be at all surprised to see her parents here. She remembered how her father had tried to talk her out of it, believing she was simply rushing into a marriage, having no idea why or that Bethany and Kelly would benefit. As far as her mother and father were concerned it was a real marriage in every sense. Would they really want to miss that?

'It is time,' Niesha said, coming to stand before her, and Tiffany still couldn't shake off that feeling that this woman knew something about the marriage deal. She always had a superior expression on her beautiful face. Had Jafar told anyone other than his aide that this was a business deal? Did anyone else know it was an arranged marriage with a difference? That he'd hired his bride?

'It is.' Tiffany took a deep breath, reassuring

herself that all brides were nervous as they were about to walk down the aisle to their future husband and these woman would expect nothing less.

'There is one more essential item.' Niesha's voice had hardened with disapproval. 'A final surprise from your soon-to-be husband.'

Niesha turned and gestured someone forward. Her father. Guilt rushed over her again for not having told anyone other than Bethany and Lilly the truth about the marriage, but she was so pleased to see him and her feelings towards the man she was to marry softened a little more.

'So you are going through with it?' The tone of her father's voice left her in no doubt he hadn't changed his mind. As far as he was concerned, she was making a big mistake.

'I am, yes.' She kept her tone firm. She had to make him think this was the real thing for her. 'This is what I want, Dad.'

'And nobody is pressuring you into this?' Had he any idea just how close he was coming to the truth?

'No,' she laughed softly, hoping to distract him, for Bethany's sake. 'Nobody is making me do anything I don't want to do.'

'In that case, you have my blessing.' He smiled and offered her his arm.

Tiffany looked at Niesha, who was watching them closely, eyes narrowed with suspicion, and she tried to derail the conversation before it deepened. 'Thank you.'

'Your mother is here too, I'm told.' Her father's lips set into a firm line once he'd informed her of his ex-wife's presence, reminding Tiffany of another reason why she'd never wanted to get married. At least not for real. If her parents could barely be civil to one another since their divorce, what was the future for her and Jafar in three months' time?

'We must not keep His Highness waiting any longer.' Niesha cut the conversation quickly. 'Nobody *ever* keeps the ruler of Shamsumara waiting.'

'Then I am ready.' Tiffany took a deep breath and looked ahead of her at the tall, ornate doors, behind which guests were assembled—and Jafar waited.

Slowly the doors opened and she stood looking into a room filled with women in black *abayas* over colourful dresses on one side and men dressed in white robes on another. Jafar stood waiting for her on a raised dais and all eyes in the hall were on her as she walked towards him on her father's arm. She, however, couldn't take her eyes from Jafar.

Dressed from head to foot in a subtle gold colour, he looked like a warrior prince. At his side hung a sword and from either side of the shoulders of his clothing, which had hints of Western influence, were fine gold chains and diamonds. As she drew closer the fine gold fabric of his headdress shone in the shaft of light that slanted down from the highest windows of the banqueting hall.

Was it a good omen or a bad one?

Her step faltered but she couldn't take her gaze from the handsome man in front of her, now so very close yet so utterly unreachable. His stubble-covered jaw flexed and she knew he was biting down hard in that way she'd already seen him do many times. Was he having the same misgivings as she was? The same doubt?

He smiled and relief surged through her as it reached his eyes, softening the hard lines of his face—and her heart. It thumped wildly and a host of butterflies took flight inside her, making her light-headed.

She let go of her father's arm and began to walk towards him again and as she reached the steps up to the dais, he moved towards her, took her hand and drew her up. Behind her there were a few gasps and she wondered if he should have done that, if he should have touched her before they were legally married.

It was then that she noticed he held a single flower. Large and white like an exotic orchid. Just as she was wondering why, he held it out to her with a smile. Once again, he was so good at acting the role of enamoured bridegroom that she could almost believe the smile was real. She took the orchid in her free hand, glad that her small but exquisite bouquet wasn't large, and lifted it up, wanting to smell the scent of the flower.

'You must put it in your bouquet,' he said softly, as if he only wanted her to hear.

She did as he asked and slipped it among her flowers, many of which she'd never seen before, and then looked back up at him, trying to chase away the nerves that were rampaging through her right now. Behind her were Lilly, Bethany and Kelly and in the assembled guests, she now knew, was her mother. What would she have to say about this arrangement? Not that it mattered now; Tiffany had gone too far, committed herself completely. She was doing this for her sister and right now nothing else mattered. She'd been paid a large sum of money for these three months and that would ensure that, not only were Bethany and Kelly free of all the threat of financial ruin, but she could set herself up again.

Lilly's advice rushed back at her as Jafar smiled at her, making her heart leap wildly. Was it the thought that she wanted more than the kiss they'd shared at the Eiffel Tower restaurant? That other than Jafar refusing her, reminding her she'd stated the marriage was in name only, there was no reason she couldn't be his true wife? That she could enjoy this time with him without the worry of future commitment or false promises?

The idea of being his sent a ripple of awareness all over her and she blushed at the thought.

'Now we can be married.' Jafar's words wiped out all those thoughts and she looked at the two ornately carved gold chairs, placed like a medieval banquet in the centre of the dais overlooking the assembled guests. The chanting of a man, dressed in white robes with a gold sash adorning them, was the official words that would join them in marriage and once the rings were exchanged the deal would be sealed in the most unbreakable way.

She would be Jafar's wife.

He led her to the chairs and she took her place as best she could in the voluminous folds of white diamond-encrusted silk. She tried hard to remember all she'd been told about what was now happening and watched as drinks were passed out to the guests in preparation for the toasting of the bride and groom.

Then Jafar took her hand. ‘Now the rings.’

Tiffany looked down at her right hand, onto which Niesha had told her to put her engagement ring in readiness. Once Jafar took the ring and placed it on her left hand and she had done the same to the gold ring he wore on his right hand, they would be married. A hired bride but a legal wife.

His fingers were warm as he slid the pink diamond from her finger and she looked up, instantly realising it was a mistake. That spark arced between them again and, together with memories of the kiss at the Eiffel Tower, heated her body. Try as she might she couldn’t look away, not even when his eyes became the darkest of greens. He took her left hand without breaking eye contact and she felt the ring being slid onto her third finger.

She was so enrapt by his heady gaze that she forgot what should happen next. He prompted her, his voice deep and husky. 'Now you must do the same.'

She blushed beneath the intensity in his eyes and focused her attention on doing what was expected. She took his right hand and eased the gold ring from his finger. Foolishly she looked up at him. The spark of desire in his eyes made her breath catch and for a moment all she could do was look at him. Then she felt him remove his right hand and replace it with the other.

She blinked back her confusion, caused by the swell of heady desire and passion tossing her around like a small ship on a stormy sea. There was the promise of quieter waters, of gentleness if she was brave enough to take it. Lilly's advice floated through her mind once more and she swallowed down the cocktail of emotions and concentrated on completing the ritual that would bind them together in marriage.

The man in the white robes chanted more loudly and applause came from the guests. 'We are now married. You are my Queen.'

* * *

Jafar had called on all his control and stayed firm against the powerful surge of desire that had raged inside him as Tiffany had slid his ring from his right hand and onto his left, making her legally his wife—his Queen.

Right now, as he looked at her, oblivious to anyone around them, he wanted to kiss her, to taste her lips against his. He wanted to feel the same heated passion as he had in Paris and he wished now he'd insisted on inserting many more Western influences into their ceremony, because then he'd have had an excuse to kiss her. Instead he would have to wait until they were alone in their suite, and after the kiss in the Eiffel Tower he wasn't sure he could risk kissing her. Not when she'd made it clear, despite the attraction between them, that she didn't want a physical relationship. As much as he wanted to kiss her again he couldn't, not when she threatened his control so completely it was unnerving and exciting at the same time.

Her lips parted as she looked up at him, inviting him with eyes as blue as the depths of the ocean, currents of passion swirling in them. Would she welcome his kiss again? The darkening of her eyes told him one thing but the tenseness of her body told him the opposite. Was that because she was fighting the desire or because she wished she weren't here doing this, that there had been some other way to help out her sister?

'We are now married.' He kept his voice firm, shutting down the desire that pulsed inside him, demanding satisfaction. 'The celebrations will continue for a few hours, then most guests will leave and we will be escorted to the Royal Suite and, as the tradition of Shamsumara dictates when a ruler marries, we will be shut in and guards will be placed at the main doors to the suite.'

'We were alone for a week in Paris. We coped then,' she said, her lashes lowering and a hint of a blush creeping over her cheeks, making her freckles, or sun kisses as he now thought of them, stand out. 'I am sure we can manage in the vastness of our suite here in the palace.'

Right at this moment he didn't think he could manage to ignore the desire even if he banished her to another country. He wanted her, desired her. His body craved hers in a way that heated his blood, pushing his legendry control to new limits, testing his honour. She looked up at him, so cool, so aloof that he would give anything to find the passionate woman he'd kissed as they'd viewed Paris from the Eiffel Tower and this time he wanted more than a kiss—much more.

'You do not find it strange?'

'That we will effectively be locked in? No. I accept that your country will do many things differently and, after all, nobody needs to know what happens—or doesn't happen between us.'

The noise level of the celebrations increased, giving him the opportunity to talk more without being overheard. 'Being shut away in our suite, with a guard at the door, is part of a long-standing tradition to secure the future heir for the kingdom. The flower I gave you is a symbol of fertility and, as part of the service, was blessed before you entered the hall. It is these traditions that mean we will have to remain married for two years, as the marriage will be assumed to have been consummated.'

'What about your word as leader of the kingdom? Wouldn't that be good enough?'

'Nobody will believe otherwise, Tiffany. Not when you are a beautiful woman and especially not with my reputation.' There was amusement in his voice and she followed his lead, allowing herself to relax.

'Ah, yes, the playboy prince,' she teased. Jafar was pleased to see the light-hearted girl he'd talked with in the English garden on a Sunday morning was beginning to emerge.

'Precisely and on top of that we have acted the part of lovers since the engagement was announced. Two years is what we agreed, but you only need to stay in Shamsumara for three months, or until my sister's baby is born.'

'No pressure, then.' She laughed and something softened inside him. He liked her sense of humour, liked how she handled all that was being thrown at her. Just as she had done in Paris, when she'd been instructed in the many traditions that she would have to adhere to while living as his wife, the Queen of Shamsumara.

Behind them there was movement as the door closed and the key turned in the lock. She was alone with her husband and the attraction and desire Tiffany had for him threatened everything she'd promised herself since she'd agreed to be his hired bride. The bridal suite was in almost subdued darkness, lit by many lanterns, their flickering flames creating a romantic ambiance, which was reflected in the Eastern music subtly filling the warm night air. The scent of incense completed the mood perfectly.

This was her wedding night. The night she'd always thought she'd give her virginity to the man she'd spend the rest of her life with. Instead she was with a man she would only spend three months with, yet that made no difference to the heady desire she had for him and she found herself wishing this could truly be her wedding night—

the night she gave herself to the desert sheikh. A night of complete fantasy.

'Do you require help with your dress?' Jafar spoke, shattering her thoughts until they resembled the hundreds of sparkling stars in the night sky beyond the ornate arched windows.

'That would be a good idea if one of the ladies is available. Or Lilly?' The thought of being able to speak with her friend fired a jolt of excitement through her. Lilly would know just what advice to give. It might not be what she herself wanted to hear, but she would tell her straight exactly what she thought she should do.

He raised his brows in amused disbelief, taking away that hardened expression he'd worn for most of the wedding celebrations. 'We are totally alone, Tiffany, and you will have to make do with me.'

'Oh.' Shock jolted her from her thoughts. As she moved across the marble floor the silk of her dress rustled and she knew there was no way she was ever coming out of it without some help.

Her heart pounded hard. Could she trust herself to allow him close, to touch her?

'You have my word that nothing will happen.' His voice lowered, becoming silky smooth. 'Unless you want it to.'

*Unless you want it to.*

Did he know that was her deepest and most secret wish? That she wanted something to happen—wanted him?

'I just want to take this dress off.' She reached up to unpin the veil.

'No, wait.' He crossed the room, bringing him unbearably close. 'I have wanted to do this since you stepped up onto the dais with me.'

She held her breath as he raised his hands and unpinned the veil from her hair. His gaze locked with hers as he let it float to the floor. Had she imagined the crackle of the spark that jumped between them?

'And this too.' He pulled the few pins from her hair and it tumbled around her shoulders, the music swaying her mind into a turmoil of passion-infused thoughts.

She should back away from the temptation he was putting before her. She wanted to be kissed again as she had been in Paris. Only this time she knew she wouldn't want it to stop. She wanted to forget everything for tonight—every bit of their deal. Was he just entertaining himself and tormenting her or did he want her as much as she wanted him?

He held her hair, focusing on it, and she backed away a little, forcing him to let go. She should ask him to unbutton the back of her dress, then she could slip away, go and hide in one of the other rooms of the suite. Get as far away from the temptation of this man as she could.

She turned her back on him. 'Can you unbutton the dress, please?' With a flutter of anticipation she lifted her hair in readiness. Seconds ticked by and the tension in the air ratcheted up to unbearable levels until eventually she heard Jafar move closer again. His touch was gentle as he began to unbutton the first of the many small buttons down her back.

Tiffany's breathing deepened as she waited,

head lowered, holding her hair against her neck. As more of the buttons were opened her nerves rose and her heart thumped, nearly skittering out of control when his fingers brushed her bare back.

Jafar paused.

She waited. The anticipation of the moment was almost too much, then he continued his task until the bodice of the dress loosened slightly around her and she became acutely aware of the fact that she was braless.

'I can manage now.' Her voice had become a husky whisper and she didn't dare move in case his fingers touched her skin again. She didn't think she could tolerate this much more. It was sheer torture.

'There are more yet.' His cracked whisper only added to the sensation of being close to him, feeling his touch on her skin or the pressure as the bodice of the dress moved when he unbuttoned yet another small white button.

Lilly's advice was all she could think about now. Would he reject her, push her away as he had done in Paris, if she told him she wanted to be kissed again or would he kiss her—and more?

'Do you feel it too?' The whispered question was out before she could stop it.

Again he paused in his task, this time holding the bodice of the dress taut at her lower back. 'The desire?'

'Yes.' That one word was so husky, so full of emotion she hardly recognised it as coming from her lips.

'More than you can imagine.'

'Would it be so wrong to give in to it?' Her nerves almost failed her as she asked the question in a whisper. 'When tonight is like a fantasy?'

Silence came back at her and she was glad she couldn't see him, see the expression on his face. What kind of fool was she? He'd been acting the part of lover all along in order to portray their marriage as real. He wasn't really interested in her.

'Is it what you really want?' The deep sensual tone of his voice sent a ripple of awareness cascading over her.

‘I’m sorry.’ She pulled away from him and walked towards the window, desperate not to look into his face, to see the shock in his handsome features. ‘I shouldn’t have said anything. I’m not used to being in situations like this.’

‘Are you referring to wedding nights or seducing a man?’ Was that a hint of amusement in his tone?

She turned to face him, a shy smile on her lips. ‘Both.’

‘That pleases me.’ He moved towards her again, coming to stand next to her at the window, looking out at the night sky as if it held the answer to her question.

She looked up at him just as he turned to her. There was no mistaking the desire that darkened his eyes, even for a woman as inexperienced as she was. ‘It does?’

‘Tiffany, you must know I want nothing more than to make love to you—tonight. Our wedding night. I want this night to be real in every sense of the word.’

Her heart thumped so hard she had to lean

against the cool marble of the arched window. He wanted her—really wanted her.

'You need to know—' she began, aware that she had to tell him now she was a virgin. She wasn't, after all, his true bride and if he was expecting experience he would be very disappointed.

'There is nothing I need to know.' He cut across her nervous words as he moved closer, pulling her to him. 'Other than you want me to make love to you, to make you truly my wife, my Queen.'

'I want that.' Those words were a husky whisper, but he didn't wait to hear more as his lips claimed hers in a kiss that was gentle yet demanding in equal measures. The desire she'd tried so hard to ignore leapt to life, sending heat spiralling through her.

She wound her arms around his neck, pulling herself against the gold silk fabric of his wedding outfit, and as his hand slipped inside the open back of her dress to caress her skin she gasped in pleasure. He kissed down her neck as the passion increased and she knew she had to try again to tell him she had no idea what to expect or what to do to please him.

'Jafar,' she gasped, which had the effect of increasing his desire, his assault on her senses. 'Jafar, I need to tell you…'

His lips trailed kisses back to her face, back to her lips and he whispered against them. 'Then tell me, because very soon I will be incapable of processing anything. You are driving me wild.'

'I'm—' she began but his kiss smothered the word. She pushed her hands against his chest and forced him to look at her. 'I'm a virgin, Jafar.'

Jafar's senses reeled. His bride, his wife, the woman he wanted to claim in a passionate frenzy was a virgin? Had he heard correctly? It should have doused the desire, calmed the passion, but it only intensified it.

She was giving herself, her most precious gift, to him and on their wedding night—their fake wedding night. It should change everything. He couldn't knowingly take her virginity, then divorce her in two years' time. *This isn't a conven-*

*tional marriage*, he reminded himself, his sense of honour slipping away into the mists of desire. *This is a business deal.* A contract they had both willingly entered into and, more than that, she was as attracted to him as he was to her.

'I'm not the kind of man who takes a woman's virginity. I'm not worthy of such a gift.' Harshness had entered his voice but the tension in his body softened when she looked up at him and smiled.

'It's very chivalrous that you care enough to try and dissuade me, but it's not going to change my mind. This is my wedding night, after all.' There was an element of coyness in her voice, which barely concealed the steely determination.

He touched his hand to her face, a stab of lust shooting through him as she closed her eyes and sighed. She was so beautiful, so incredibly sexy, and the fact that she now wanted the marriage to be real, tonight at least, filled him with hope. Maybe their time together would be much more pleasurable than he'd ever imagined.

Lust and desire careered around him and he

couldn't take much more. His body was almost exploding with need for this woman and the fact that she would be completely his only intensified that. 'Are you certain this is what you want?'

'Tonight, with you, is everything I want.' She moved towards him, reaching up and placing her lips on his in a gentle, teasing way. 'I want the fantasy of you, this room, everything.'

He wanted to deepen the kiss, to demand so much from her, but he had a duty to her. He wanted to make sure this first experience of sex was the most pleasurable she'd ever experienced and he couldn't do that if he lost control now.

## CHAPTER SEVEN

THE SOFTNESS OF Jafar's kiss was so intoxicating Tiffany's mind spun, leaving her light-headed, and she leant against his lean, hard body. There was no question in her mind that she was doing the right thing. She wanted his kiss, his touch, his total possession in a way she'd never known before. The need inside her for this man, her husband, was all-consuming.

When he stopped kissing her she looked up at him, wondering if he was about to tell her he didn't want her, that a woman without any sexual experience didn't interest him. She searched his eyes, now so dark, looking for some hint to what he was feeling.

'I am honoured that you have chosen me as your first lover.' His voice was as soft as the silk dress she wore and it caressed her senses so gently, easing the nerves that surely went with such a momentous event. 'I want to make this night special for you.'

'Being here, with you, in this wonderful palace, it is already a special night.' She looked beyond him towards the large bed, draped in gold silk. A trail of lanterns created the ultimate romantic bedroom for a bride and groom while the remainder of the room was shrouded in darkness.

Without a word, he took her hand and led her away from the window and the warm night air, through the archway that led to the bedroom. The vastness of the domed ceiling was overpowering—or was it the enormity of what she was doing? She hesitated and he turned to her.

'It is a tradition that those attending the bride leave suitable gifts to be opened after the ceremony and your friend and sister have done that.' The gentleness in his voice wasn't reflected in his eyes as the passion and desire she'd seen before she'd told him she was a virgin returned, obliterating everything. He gestured to the ornately decorated table that stood alone at one side of the room.

She could see several gifts, all neatly packaged with white tissue paper and gold ribbon. 'Should I open them now?'

'You may do if you so wish, but I would rather continue with the task I started a few moments ago.' The suggestive rise of his brows made a heavy sensation deep inside her at the thought of him not only unbuttoning her dress, but removing it.

She moved towards him, lulled by the soft music, the heady scent on the warm night air. Everything was all so perfect. How could she not want to make the most of this moment? He watched her intently as she smiled coyly at him, then slowly she turned her back to him, waiting for him to unbutton the remainder of the buttons, only this time she longed for his fingers to brush over her skin, to set her alight with desire.

She pulled her loose hair over her shoulder and waited with building anticipation to feel the bodice of her dress move as he dealt with the buttons.

His touch when it came was the sensual trail of his fingers down her spine, making her shudder with pleasure.

'You are so beautiful.' His husky whisper was filled with desire and she closed her eyes against the onslaught of sensations she'd never felt before. 'I want to explore all of you. Slowly. Very slowly.'

She clutched her hair tighter as her control slipped away, thawing her virginal body like the sun rising over a frost-covered landscape of England, bathing it in the heat of the desert sun. She sensed him move closer, her body tuned into his every move, anticipating his touch. The kiss he pressed against her bare shoulder forced a sigh of pleasure from her lips and she moved her head to one side as he kissed up her neck.

'I want to show you the wonders of making love,' he whispered in her ear before kissing back down her neck.

'Show me,' she responded in a throaty whisper, wondering if that seductive voice was really her.

He pulled her against him, her partially bare

back pressing against the gold silk of his wedding robes, feeling the hardness of the diamonds that decorated them. She turned to look at him as his arms circled her waist. Then his lips claimed hers and she stretched her body, needing to deepen the kiss, to show him how much she wanted him, wanted this.

A harsh stream of words tore from him as he broke the kiss and she could feel his chest rising and falling as rapidly as hers. Was he angry? Uncertainty threatened. 'What's wrong?'

'How can anything be wrong with a woman like you in my arms?' He gently pushed her forward, turned her round and she was about to step away when she felt him working on the last of the bodice buttons.

Jafar forced himself to control the fierce passion surging through him. The need to rip the dress from her, take her to the bed and claim her was so fierce, so intense, he'd had to focus hard on those damn buttons. Who the hell put so many buttons on a wedding dress?

'Now I will finish what I started.' As the last of the buttons were freed he stood and looked at her back, his gaze trailing down her sexy spine as he willed his body to slow the pace, forced his needs back under control.

He slid his hands inside the dress and around her waist, feeling the silk begin to move, to slip away. In a slow purposeful move his hands massaged up her sides, then up over her shoulder blades and finally he pushed away the shoulders of the modest wedding dress that had never really concealed her fabulous figure from him.

Tiffany pressed her arms against her, allowing the sleeves to slide downwards, exposing the full glory of her naked back. His breathing was hard and laboured and he took a deep controlling breath, resisting the urge to push the silk away from her hips to reveal more of her.

*Patience.*

In a bid to hold onto his control, to take things slowly, he moved his fingertips down her back. The shudder of pleasure and soft sigh she gave was almost too much, but he held onto his control. Instead he put his arms around her waist, spreading his palms over her bare stomach before moving upwards to her naked breasts. He caressed the swell of them, desire throbbing through him as she leant back against him, gasping in pleasure. He circled the hardness of her nipples with his fingertips, lowering his head to kiss her neck once more.

Her scent, the same intoxicating one he'd noticed before, pushed his desire higher, as did the taste of her skin on his lips.

'Jafar,' she sighed his name as he kissed up her neck, his fingers still teasing her nipples.

*Slowly.*

The word pulsed through him and again he moved away from her, his hands lingering on her waist briefly before he pushed the silk dress down until it billowed out around her legs in a mass of white and sparkling diamonds. The white panties she wore accentuated her pert bottom.

'So beautiful.' His throaty words warned him again he was in danger of losing control, of giving into passion far too quickly. 'Turn round.'

Slowly she turned, the silk of the dress still around her lower legs, the brightness of the white reminding him of her virginal body, waiting to be claimed—by him. He took her hand, helping her to step out from the dress, unable to take his eyes off her long, slender legs as she did so.

Without breaking eye contact he led her away from the puffed-up silk of the dress and towards the vast bed. The sound of her heeled shoes on the marble floor was wonderfully erotic. She was naked apart from the white panties and heeled shoes and so sexy, so beautiful.

'I don't know where to begin with your robes.' The demure tone of her voice was in complete contrast to the image she created as she stood next to the silk-covered bed, the glow of the candles caressing her pale skin.

She wanted to undress him? The idea sent his body into overdrive and all he could think about was lying naked with her, seeing her pale skin next to the darkness of his. He unclipped the gold decorations at the collar of his wedding robe.

'It is much easier than removing you from your

gown,' he teased as he moved towards her, his robe open at the neck. He held the fabric towards her. 'Pull this.'

Her eyes were wide and full of desire, her delicious breasts rising and falling with each breath as she reached out to take the gold fabric from him, her fingers brushing his. 'Like this?'

The question was teasing and slowly she pulled, a provocative smile of satisfaction on her lips as she exposed his chest, her gaze lingering on him, scorching his skin. He pointed to the fastening inside the robe at his waist. 'And then this here.'

She pulled the fastening and the gold robes slithered down him like a serpent so that he too now wore only underwear. Unlike Tiffany, he didn't stand in the gold silk robe, but kicked it casually aside, along with the soft leather sandals fashioned especially for his wedding.

'Now we are equal.' She bit her lower lip and looked at him coyly from beneath long lashes.

'Not quite.' Jafar lowered himself to his knees at her feet and ran his hands down her legs, over her knees and to her shapely ankles. 'These need to go.'

She lifted her foot and he slid the shoe from her, placing it on the floor as he looked up at her. Then, before his lust got the better of him, he let her foot go and did the same again, this time tossing the shoe aside as he began to stand up, pausing to press a kiss, first on her thigh, then on her stomach, then upwards to her breasts. Wild fire erupted in him as he took one nipple in his mouth, nipping at it.

'Oh,' Tiffany cried as she pressed her fingers into his hair and he moved to the other breast and began the torment once more.

He moved his kisses lower again and looked up at her, knowing he couldn't take much more of this. His control was slipping rapidly away. He took the fine lace of her panties and pulled them down her legs, resisting the urge to rip them from her and push her back onto the bed and cover her body with his. She stepped out of the skimpy lace and he kissed her thigh, moving upwards towards the very centre of her femininity, lingering there as he kissed the softness of her skin. Wanting more, wanting to taste her.

*Not yet*, he told himself.

Tiffany dragged in a deep and ragged breath as the warmth of Jafar's caressed her skin where moments ago the soft white lace of her panties had been. She stood breathing hard, wanting more than his breath on her skin. She was completely naked and so incredibly aroused she could hardly think.

Just as her legs weakened, threatening to buckle her knees, Jafar stood up, so close to her that the soft dark hair on his chest grazed her sensitised nipples. How could anyone stand this? It was exquisite and torturous at the same time. She wanted it to stop but at the same time she didn't want it to ever end.

'Lie down,' he demanded, his eyes so dark with desire they were almost black. She did as he'd bid, sitting on the edge of the massive bed, then leaning back on her elbows, watching him as if she'd been waiting for this moment with this man all her life.

He didn't take his eyes from her as he divested himself of his underwear, leaving him powerfully and wonderfully naked. His skin was olive dark, the candlelight seeming to illuminate every contour of every muscle. Hungrily she drank him in, her gaze sliding down the light covering of dark hair on his muscled chest, down over an incredibly defined flat stomach to the length of his erection.

She bit at her bottom lip, a dart of uncertainty soon chased away by the increasing beat of desire deep within her, the need to feel him intimately against her, feel him inside her, possessing her in the most natural way. Instinctively she moved herself backwards on the bed, looking directly into his eyes as he joined her, bracing the strength of his body over hers.

He kissed her, holding himself away from her, and she kissed him back, demanding more from him as she slipped her tongue inside his mouth. A wild sensation erupted within her and her hips lifted to him, seeking the release she knew only he could give, the release she wanted so badly that she was losing her mind, losing her ability to think.

A wild flurry of words she didn't understand unleashed from him as he broke the kiss, looking almost out of control as his body remained tantalisingly over hers. What had he just said? The question flew from her mind as he began the torment on her nipple again and she let her head fall back onto the silk covers, sighing softly and giving herself up to the pleasure of his kisses. He moved to the other nipple, making her body wriggle, then he moved lower again.

She gasped out loud, her eyes flying wide as she felt his tongue caress her intimately. His fingers gripped her thighs as he continued the torment, making her body buck and writhe, taking her to heights of pleasure she'd never imagined possible.

Just when she thought she was going to break apart, to shatter into hundreds of tiny pieces, he began kissing his way back up her body. This time his was much closer to her and as if her body had taken over she pulled up her knees, wrapping her ankles around his legs as she clung to his back. The heated hardness of his erection pressed against her, but it wasn't enough and she lifted her hips, gasping as she felt him slowly possess her.

She pressed herself provocatively up to him, drawing him deeper inside her until he completely filled her and his name came to her lips. 'Jafar.'

He looked down at her and before he could say anything, or stop, she kissed him hard, demanding more from him, from this moment. She wanted to live the fantasy to the full.

She caught the deep guttural growl that tore from him as he kissed her back, setting her on fire as he began to move inside her, deeper and harder. Everything turned wild, as she gasped against his lips, lifting herself up to him, digging her nails into his back. He thrust deeper and harder, taking her to a height of wild pleasure she'd never imagined possible.

'Tiffany.' He growled her name, followed by a rush of words she had no hope of understanding, but it only intensified the experience and she clung to him as her body began to float among the stars.

It was pure ecstasy and as she floated back down to earth, she became aware of his body, sweat slicked and hot, against hers as he lay on top of her.

With a thud of her heart the words I love you tried to force themselves past her lips, but she bit down hard to keep them in. It was just the wildness of the moment. She'd lost her virginity to a man she found compellingly attractive. It was nothing more than heated lust of the moment. It could never be more than that. She was just being fanciful.

Jafar woke as dawn stretched her fingers of soft orange light across the desert sky. His body was heavy with the effects of last night and with a smile of satisfaction he recalled the moment Tiffany had kissed him from his sleep in the early hours and they had once more enjoyed one another's bodies as hot passion had ruled over them.

He moved in the vastness of the bed, expecting to find her naked body, but the bed was empty. He sat up and looked around the almost dark room, the candles having long since gone out. She was standing by the ornate table, dressed in one of the two gold robes left for them and holding one of the gifts he'd suggested her sister and friend leave for her, as would normally happen to a bride in Shamsumara—especially a royal bride.

'According to our tradition you should have opened them last night,' he said, a teasing note in his voice as he flung back the covers, got out of bed, pulled on the other pale gold robe and walked over to her.

She turned to face him and smiled. She looked different. A night spent in his bed had given a glow to her pale skin, accentuating the freckles he found so irresistible. 'I was otherwise occupied last night.'

Her bashful words made him smile, as did the memory of just how occupied they had been.

When he'd agreed to this deal with her, he'd never expected his wedding night would have been what it became. A hot passionate night, the like of which he'd never known before—ever.

He moved behind her, pulling her against him as his body stirred, demanding satisfaction from this woman once more. 'We could be occupied again. In fact, we have a whole week in which to occupy ourselves.'

She laughed softly, a very sexy sound, and he pressed a kiss to the side of her neck, feeling the zing of passion rising between them. 'I have gifts to open first.'

First? He liked the sound of that, the promise of once again taking her to his bed. He watched as she opened the first gift, a beautiful necklace with a heart pendant. Her slender fingers trembled slightly as she opened the heart locket to reveal a small photo of her sister and niece.

'Shall I fasten it on for you?' He could feel the mood dip. She must be thinking of home and all she'd left behind.

'Yes, please.' Her soft whisper was almost too

much for him as he took the necklace from her and she lifted her hair, just as she had done last night when he unbuttoned her wedding dress. After he'd fastened it he stroked his fingers down her neck and along her shoulders, feeling the heat of her skin beneath the silk wrap.

'Open the other and then I will call for breakfast.' What he really wanted was to pick her up and take her back to his bed, but sense prevailed.

She leant forward and picked up the remaining gift from the ornate table, pulling at the gold ribbon and then opening the white tissue to reveal a beautiful box. He kissed her neck as she opened the box, the idea of breakfast slipping to the back of his mind. Indulging in a more passionate activity would be far more satisfying.

Tiffany gasped with shock, snapped the box shut and pulled away from him, leaving him momentarily wondering what was happening. 'Is it not a suitable gift?'

He had made it clear to her sister and her friend it was tradition for the bridesmaids to leave gifts for the bride that would help her in her new role as a wife. The necklace was perfect, forming a connection with her homeland. What was in the box that would upset her so much?

Her beautifully arched brows pulled together and the look on her face was one of genuine fear. What the hell was in that box?

'It's a very suitable gift. I only wish I had opened it last night.'

'What is it?' he demanded sharply.

She looked down at the box clutched in her hand, then handed it to him, her expression wary, as if she was expecting an explosion of fury from him at any minute. He took it roughly from her, opened it and swore savagely in his own tongue. Inside was a box of condoms with a note attached.

*Have some fun! Xx*

'Condoms?' The word was fired out from him and a cold slick of dread crept over him. He *never* slept with a woman without using protection. Even if she told him she was on the pill, he always used condoms. *Always*, damn it.

'I didn't think…' Her words trailed away as she pushed her hands through her hair in frustration. He wanted to be angry, with her, with himself, but the distress she showed made that impossible—especially after last night.

'It is my fault. I should have been more responsible. You told me you were a virgin. I should have made sure I looked after you—in every way.'

He moved to take her in his arms and held her against him, inhaling the scent of her hair as the ramifications of what could happen settled over him. Last night they could have done the one thing he'd sworn never to do. They could have created a new life.

'But what if…?' she said as her breath shuddered from her. 'What if I'm pregnant?'

He closed his eyes against the word, knowing full well that if this had happened in Paris they could have averted an unwanted pregnancy. Things were very different here in Shamsumara, especially for the Sheikh and his Queen in the days after their wedding. 'There is nothing we can do now. We must spend the week together, as tradition dictates. We cannot be apart for any reason.'

'But a baby, Jafar,' she implored, looking so frightened his heart constricted. 'That would change everything.'

He took a deep breath, silently acknowledging the truth of what she'd just said. 'It was one night, Tiffany. Your first time.'

He didn't believe a word of what he'd just said, but put as much conviction into it as he could. The blame for this lay firmly at his feet and if anyone was going to spend the next few weeks worrying, it was him.

Tiffany tried to eat the delicious breakfast that had been prepared for them, and the fragrant tea smelt amazing, but the worry of last night wouldn't go away, despite Jafar's apparent lack of concern. She might have been a virgin when she'd walked in this room last night, but she knew that one time was all it took.

Had his subtle yet persistent seduction been

part of a bigger plan? Had she fallen into the trap of believing all he'd told her about his family situation? What if his plan had been to seduce her, create the heir he needed? If so, what would happen to her now?

'You should try and eat something.' He spoke firmly as he looked across at her, the lover of last night disappearing as the sun rose higher in the bright blue sky.

'Why didn't your sister come to our wedding?' The question rushed from her as doubts stacked up along with the realisation that his sister hadn't been present at yesterday's ceremony. Did she really exist? And, if so, did she really carry the heir Jafar needed to rule his kingdom?

'She is heavily pregnant, carrying the heir not only for her husband's kingdom but for Shamsumara. Travelling was out of the question.' He poured the tea from the most ornate gold pot she'd ever seen into small glasses, also lavishly decorated with gold. 'Once our week of observing the tradition of being alone has passed, I will escort you to meet her.'

Tiffany took the tea from him, inhaling the delicate scent, and sipped at the sweetness of the liquid, still trying to decide if last night had been planned or if they had both been taken by surprise by the strength of the desire between them. It had certainly been that way for her and, with her feelings towards Jafar deepening, despite knowing it was foolish, she'd hoped it was the same for him.

'But our marriage isn't real. Wouldn't that just complicate everything?' Why had she said that? Meeting his sister would be the perfect way to discover if she'd fallen into some bizarre scheme to rule his kingdom.

'You're right.' The sharpness of the declaration cut through her unease, causing more doubt to rise in her mind. 'In the circumstances, maybe it would be better if I went alone?'

If that didn't confirm she was nothing more than a temporary and necessary addition to his life, then nothing did. Whatever misguided affection she was beginning to feel for him, it was not reciprocated in any way.

* * *

Tiffany had to remind herself of this every night for the next week. As soon as the sun slipped down behind the sand dunes, Jafar became the passionate lover he'd been on their wedding night once again and, just like that first night, she was powerless to resist. He confused her and made her fall deeper and harder for him every night.

Last night, their final night together as newlyweds, the passion had been more powerful than ever and the lovemaking so intense, but, just as they had been doing since she'd opened Lilly's gift, they had used protection. Not that it lessened the worry that she might already be carrying his child—a child he'd claimed he didn't ever want. A child that would complicate everything in a way she couldn't bear to consider.

Now the sun was rising, heating the cool palace rooms in which she had been shut away from the world with this man for seven days and nights. She had no idea what to expect when he resumed his normal daily life, or even what that would be for her.

'I have duties to return to today,' he said, as if he'd read her mind, and she turned to see him fully robed in white, looking as magnificent as ever. 'You too will have duties to learn and my aide will help with these. He has been setting up your suggested charity since our wedding.'

There was no mistaking the aloofness in his voice, or the tense way he stood, as if he couldn't wait to leave her, to go back to his life. A kick of pain shot through her. They'd just enjoyed the most amazing week, where passion had ruled everything, and now he was going to turn his back on her.

'Good,' she said sharply. 'I will need something to do for the next, what is it now, eleven weeks?' If that didn't serve as a reminder of their deal, then nothing would.

He scowled at her and his anger simmered across the increasing heat in the room. 'You are counting the weeks until you leave so exactly?'

'Of course, I am.' Her flippant tone helped to instil confidence in her, to give her the same carefree attitude he had adopted.

He came to stand before her, his eyes vibrant, sparking with anger. 'Have you not found pleasure in your first week?'

*Pleasure.* She'd found far more than pleasure. She'd become ensnared in the web of passion he'd weaved every night and had no idea how she was ever going to sleep alone again. Already her body longed for his, longed for his touch and so much more.

Jafar looked at Tiffany as she stood in the fine silk clothes he'd ordered for her arrival. The matching headscarf clutched in her hand, the tightness of her fingers giving away so much more than her blasé words. He knew then that whatever it was they'd shared, that undeniable spark of sexual attraction would now have to come to an end. This was the business side of their deal, and the distraction they'd found in one another, while adhering to the tradition of remaining solely in each other's company for a week, now had to be put aside. He had to do all he could to prevent Simdan from making a claim on Shamsumara and until his sister's child, his heir, was born, that claim could come at any time.

He seriously doubted that he would be able to resist Tiffany each night, but it must be done. This wasn't a real marriage. It was a deal to save his kingdom and nothing more. She was a bride he'd hired at considerable cost. She wasn't even one of his affairs. Passion and desire must be put aside.

*You took her virginity.*

The accusing words thrashed around his mind. Not least of all because he should never have done that and, worse still, should have ensured that the necessary precautions were used. How the hell had he been remiss about such a thing, when every other time he'd had sex with a woman he'd always been obsessively careful? After the example of marriage he'd witnessed growing up between his cold father and his fragile mother, he'd vowed he would never have a child unless it was born into a loving union. That was, of course, when he'd been nothing more than the spare heir, before he'd inherited the right to rule over Shamsumara after his brother's tragic death. Would his plans to make his sister's child his heir be enough to keep Simdan at bay?

'Pleasure was not part of our deal, Jafar.' Her determined tone forced his mind from the tragedy of the past, back to the present, back to the situation they now found themselves in.

'Neither was a child.' The hurt expression on her face jolted him and he schooled his frustration at the situation he was now in. 'Forgive me. That was uncalled for.'

He reached out to her, but she pulled back. 'I hope that very soon I can reassure you that will not be an issue. In the meantime, I would like to sleep alone from now on.'

'As you wish.' A fierce sense of rejection rushed over him. Never before had a woman made it so blatantly clear that she no longer desired him. He'd always called time on his affairs. 'I have much to keep me from our marital bed and, as you will be leaving after the agreed three months, it will convincingly build the story that you are unhappy here with me.'

# CHAPTER EIGHT

THE LAST THING Tiffany wanted to do was parade herself in front of the guests assembled at the gift ceremony, especially when she discovered that Niesha would once again be attending. There was still that feeling there was something, some kind of history, between Niesha and Jafar. Whatever had happened between them, Tiffany was sure that Niesha believed it wasn't over.

The hours passed slowly and Tiffany could barely recall the food she'd eaten or half of the gifts she'd been given. Most of the guests had now left, leaving her and Jafar with his aide and those who appeared to be part of his team of assistants and the ever-present Niesha and Simdan.

The music still filled the great hall and the dancers continued with their exotic entertainment, and as she watched Tiffany became acutely aware of Niesha's scrutiny. The dark-haired woman ended her conversation with another guest and made her way towards where Tiffany sat on the large red and gold cushions. Before she joined her, Niesha looked across the hall at her husband, now deep in conversation with Jafar.

Tiffany looked at Jafar and frowned. Whatever it was that he and Simdan were discussing appeared to be getting heated. Not that they were raising their voices—quite the opposite. Tiffany could tell from their body language that they were hissing and snarling at one another like jungle cats fighting over territory. She looked again at Niesha, only to find she was the object of the other woman's scrutiny and not whatever was happening between the cousins.

'I have a special gift for you.' Niesha's voice dragged her attention away from the two men, but she couldn't shake off the thought that their discussion was a direct threat to the deal she and Jafar had struck. A deal that, if she didn't honour it, would mean Jafar had the right to call back in the money he'd paid her, money that Bethany needed.

Tiffany looked at Niesha, unease spreading over her as if the woman had said or done something to threaten her. 'That is very kind of you. I'm quite overwhelmed by everyone's generosity.'

She kept her voice neutral, sure it would be unwise to let her suspicion show. Niesha smiled brightly and settled herself on the cushions next to her, presenting from the folds of her *abaya* a beautifully wrapped gift. Tiffany took it, shocked to see her hands were trembling. She opened it, to reveal a key-like object, made from gold and studded with jewels. It was most definitely not an imitation tourist trinket and she had no idea what it was or what it might represent. All she knew was that it was as real as the sun that was setting beyond the palace.

'It is the deity of love.' The smile on Niesha's lips didn't reflect in her eyes. Only cold malice showed in their inky black depths and Tiffany began to fear that her discussion with Bethany on the eve of her wedding had been overheard.

Was that why she was now being given such a gift? To show that, although the full details of the deal she'd made with Jafar weren't known, the fact that she was here as a hired bride was most certainly known. How could she have been so remiss to talk about it like that in front of others?

'It is very beautiful.' The gold was cold to the touch, but not as frosty as Niesha's expression or her icy tone. Tiffany had suspected there was once something between this woman and the man she now called her husband and somehow this gift confirmed that. Or was she being fanciful? Reading too much into things as she always did?

'It is what I would have wanted.' Niesha let the words, veiled in threat, linger between them, and the music that still played in the background suddenly seemed incredibly loud and overpowering. 'Had I been Jafar's bride.'

So that was it. Niesha and Jafar had been lovers and, judging by the venom in Niesha's words, she was still very much in love with Jafar. Tiffany's gaze darted to her husband and his cousin, who had now moved away from the remaining guests, to stand together under the archway that led to the formal palace gardens. There was no mistaking the hostility between the two men. Was it because of Niesha? She was, after all, Simdan's wife.

'The gift or love?' The response fired from Tiffany in an uncharacteristic need to protect herself, to stand her ground. She had no idea what from, she just sensed she needed to.

Niesha laughed. A cold splintering sound like iced puddles cracking in winter. The image made Tiffany momentarily homesick. She'd never see that here, but Niesha wasn't done yet. 'Love is not something Jafar will ever give a woman. He made that very clear to me, as I am sure he has to you also.'

As the warning in those words sank in, Tiffany recalled exactly what she'd wanted to say to him as the heights of passion had claimed her on her wedding night and was eternally grateful she'd bitten down on the words, kept them from tumbling out in a passionate frenzy.

What would have happened if she'd said *I love*

*you*? It would have been too late to change the mistake they'd both made, a mistake she was still waiting to find out the consequences of. Tiffany swallowed back the nausea of that thought. She couldn't be pregnant, she just couldn't, and she tried hard to take comfort in Jafar's reassurance that it had been her first time and unlikely.

As the fear of what could be lingered over her like a storm cloud ready to burst, she felt Niesha's scrutiny once more. The last thing she needed to let her see was just how unsettled the gift had made her.

'Then I thank you for your gift and hope it brings all that it should.' She kept her voice light as she looked at Jafar, who chose that moment to look across the room at her. Even from that distance her body heated and she dragged in a deep breath, forcing her emotions back under control.

Jafar had been angry beyond words as Simdan had insisted they talk about his claim to Shamsumara and had taken the conversation away from everyone. He'd been aware of the exchange between Tiffany and Niesha, seen the gift given; he had no idea what it was, but knowing Niesha it would have to be something to make her appear superior to Tiffany. As he wondered how he'd ever thought he could be married to her, he forced his mind back onto the conversation he was having with his cousin.

His cousin wanted to rule Shamsumara and still thought he had a claim on the throne. All Jafar could do now was hope all he'd put into action would be enough to stave off that threat. His marriage to Tiffany just needed to hold this man at bay until his heir was born.

'There is no claim for you to make now, Simdan,' he snapped out coldly, determined to do right by his brother's memory and retain the rule of the kingdom of Shamsumara. It might not be what he had ever envisaged for himself, but it was now his duty—and honour. 'My sister's child will provide the heir required by our laws for me to rule and my new marital status satisfies all the necessary conditions for ruler of Shamsumara.'

'Why do you need to name your sister's child

as heir?' Simdan snarled at him, his black eyes fierce with undisguised power.

'After my brother's untimely death, I want to ensure the kingdom has a successor named, one who deserves to be the ruler of Shamsumara.' He looked at the man he despised, more certain than ever that he'd had something to do with the accident that had claimed his brother's life and that of his wife. It was too much of a coincidence that he'd launched a challenge to rule over Shamsumara within days of his brother's death. Soon after that he'd ensured his claim to the throne couldn't be ignored and had married Niesha, the most calculating woman Jafar had ever had the misfortune to know, although that wasn't how he remembered her from his youth.

'And what of your charming new wife?' The threat in Simdan's voice was clear. 'Will she not provide you with your heir?'

Jafar sensed he was being toyed with, that for some reason Simdan believed he had the upper hand. 'Our marriage happened only a week ago.

It is too soon to know if our union has brought about an heir.'

He couldn't believe he was saying those words to Simdan, of all people, or how much truth was in them. What was he going to do if Tiffany was carrying his child? He'd never wanted to be a father, not after the indifference he'd known from his own while his brother, older by one year, had basked in the sunshine of his approval. He didn't ever want to be in that position. Now it seemed a very real possibility.

'You consummated your marriage?' The leer on Simdan's face made his blood run cold. 'You got more than you bargained for from your hired bride?'

Jafar clenched his fists in an effort not to grab Simdan's robes and threaten him. The disrespect he had for Tiffany was out of order, but it was the fierce need to protect the woman he'd married that alarmed him more than anything else. 'I have no idea what you are talking about.'

Simdan folded his arms across his chest and raised his chin in a display of power that would rival any of the exotic birds of Shamsumara. 'Make the most of your days as ruler, cousin, for they are numbered. I will prove your marriage is a sham.'

'If you will excuse me, I have a gift to present to my wife.' He looked across at Tiffany, to see her holding her own in conversation with Niesha. Alarm chased down his spine. If Simdan had challenged him, then almost certainly Niesha would be challenging his wife.

*His wife.*

Twice within the last few seconds she'd come to his mind as that. Not Tiffany, or his hired bride, but his wife. The week spent solely in her company must have made him weak, softened his emotions. That would have to change if he was to hold onto his position as ruler. He would never succumb to such power-reducing emotions as affection and most definitely not love. Lust and desire were all he needed.

'I am intrigued,' Simdan said as he stood by his side, watching Tiffany in a way that made Jafar's anger boil up. 'What gift will you give to a bride who will be gone within months?'

A pang of guilt shot through Jafar. The gift he intended to present her with would cast aside any doubt that their marriage was real. It would mock Simdan's meddling words that suggested his bride would be gone within months and that was exactly what he'd intended when he'd organised what had become a traditional gift for Al-Shehri men to present to their brides.

'I know what you are doing, Simdan.' Jafar's cold words slid out slowly, control and calculation in every one, but he didn't look at his cousin. 'You will never overthrow my rule no matter what wild stories you fabricate.'

As he strode away Simdan's cruel laughter followed him, but right now he had other things to worry about. Whatever it was Niesha was up to needed to be cut off. Tiffany didn't deserve to be in the firing line of his problems.

As Jafar marched across the marble floor towards her Tiffany couldn't help the sense of foreboding that filled her. The air had become heavy and tense as the few remaining guests stepped back to allow him past. It was as if a storm were brewing.

'I have one last gift for my bride,' he proclaimed to anyone who would listen, and around them curious glances were cast their way. He raised his hand in signal and a door opened to reveal Aaleyah and the most beautiful dog Tiffany had ever seen.

Then she realised what was happening. The dog was for her. Aaleyah smiled as she handed the lead to Tiffany, and even though she didn't want to, she took it and stroked the softness of the dog's head. It was a tall, lean animal, with sleek fur the colour of sand and the kindest eyes she'd ever seen. The eyes of a true friend.

'I can't have a dog.' She looked up at Jafar, imploring him to understand. She wouldn't be here long enough. It wasn't fair to the dog.

'It is a tradition started by my grandfather and one I have kept. It is a gift to show my commitment to my wife.'

She couldn't do anything but accept the gift with everyone's attention on her. Worse than that, there was that clause in the contract she'd signed, that if she revealed the truth about their marriage their deal would end. He'd have every right to take back all he'd given to Bethany and she couldn't let that happen, not now her sister was finally looking more like herself again.

The giving of the gift also seemed to be the cue for everyone to leave and, after a long day of smiling and pretending, she was once more alone with Jafar with only the dog, who had settled at her feet as if they had known each other for years.

'Her name is Leah.' Jafar spoke as she looked down at the resting dog.

'I can't keep her, Jafar.' She looked up at him as he stood over her, determined to resist the urge to stand so as not to allow him to know he intimidated her. 'What will happen when I leave? It's not fair to her.'

'That is why I opted for an adult dog, not a puppy that would bond with you.' His explanation didn't help. It ripped her fragile heart to pieces.

Was it the thought of the dog not missing her or Jafar planning for her departure?

'You shouldn't have got her at all.'

'It is tradition. One I wish to continue. My grandfather gave my grandmother a Saluki.'

She stood up quickly, causing the dog to look up with questioning eyes. 'If tradition is so important and forms such a part of our deal, I think you need to tell me a lot more than you did when we spoke in England.'

'There is nothing more you need to know.'

'If I am to keep accepting fertility gifts and symbols of love, then I think I need to know what is really going on. I need to know the truth of what is happening here between you and your cousin.'

Jafar sighed. 'Very well, but not here.'

Jafar knew, now more than ever, he owed Tiffany the full story. She had become his wife in the true sense of the word and while their deal still stood she deserved to know everything, from the part she was playing to the threat Simdan posed to Shamsumara.

He took her hand and led her into the private royal gardens, aware that already Leah was following her new mistress. This discussion should really be done in complete privacy, but he didn't trust himself not to give into the desire he still had for her, desire that should long ago have been sated but most definitely wasn't. The next best place for a private discussion was his own gardens.

'This is so beautiful.' Her voice was a silky whisper of wonder and he clenched down on the desire he had to fight if he stood any chance of achieving what their deal had been about in the first place.

The lights from the palace reflected in the still waters of the pool and around the gardens lanterns burned, casting a soft yellow light. He ignored the image she created in her cream silk dress, which clung to her body, reminding him of how it had looked in the light from the lanterns on their wedding night. Leah stood calmly beside Tiffany, completing the picture of a Shamsumarian queen.

His Queen. His wife.

*Enough.*

'This is where I always come to relax,' he said as he walked beneath the tall arches and into the luxurious garden room.

'I'm not here to relax,' she said as she joined him, Leah at her heel. 'I need to know what all this is about—this need to retain your kingdom.'

'Sit,' he commanded, smiling at the defiant tilt of her chin before she joined him on the array of colourful cushions. He was about to open himself up to a woman, to share his story with her, something he'd never done before, but after she'd shared something much more precious with him, he owed it to her.

'What happened to your brother?' Her question went right to the heart of his turmoil, threw open the door he'd tried to keep shut and brought back all the pain. He steadfastly refused to feel it and instead focused his attention on the woman he'd married as part of a deal.

He looked at her face, at the soulful expression in her blue eyes, and tried to deal with the memory of the day he'd learnt, not only had his brother lost his life, but his wife too. 'Malek was a pilot and he and his wife were on their way to her homeland when a sandstorm brought them down.'

'That is so sad.' She lowered her gaze and he didn't say anything about Simdan's part in it, how he'd failed to let anyone know even though he'd heard of the disaster. If they had found them sooner maybe none of this would be happening, but then Tiffany would never have come into his life. He'd never have known the intense desire and pleasure from making her truly his wife.

He couldn't think like that. It was a dangerous path to travel. 'They were on their way to tell her parents they were to be grandparents. Their child would have secured Malek's rule and Shamsumara's future.'

Tiffany gasped and looked at him. 'That is why you need to name your heir? To secure the future of your kingdom?'

'In part, but also because now Simdan has a son, he could make a claim for my title if I had remained unmarried. Even though I am now married, that claim is still possible as I am without an heir. In three months' time I will have an heir for the kingdom and his claim will no longer be possible.'

He wouldn't say anything about the delicate situation they too were now in after their wedding night. He had no wish to distress her further. He would follow her lead and not mention the subject—at least until sufficient time had passed to be able to determine if she was expecting his child. He sincerely hoped it was not the case. He had no wish to be responsible for a child that would one day have to follow in his footsteps and become the ruler of Shamsumara. He knew only too well what it was to be brought up with that legacy hanging over you. If he'd felt that pressure as the spare heir, how must his brother have felt?

'And if I remain here for three months, this will ensure your cousin can't do anything to claim the throne.'

'That is correct, but more importantly my people, my advisers, must believe the marriage is real. They must believe that you intend to remain my wife. That is why I gave you Leah. To add credibility to our union.'

At the mention of her name, Leah looked up at him, then, deciding there wasn't anything to gain, laid her head on her paws once more and closed her eyes. Already she was faithful to her mistress.

'There is one more thing I need to know.' He sensed Tiffany's trepidation.

'Which is?'

'What is between you and Niesha?'

Her question touched a raw nerve, and the sense of rejection after Niesha had shunned him for a better prospect came back to him. 'Niesha and I were promised to one another from a young age, as is customary in Shamsumara. As the younger son, the one who was free to build his own business instead of ruling a country, I wasn't good enough for her and she very quickly became engaged to my cousin when he became the ruler of Mirtiesa two years ago.'

'There isn't any history between you?' He could tell from the way she asked that she'd picked up on the tension between them, tension that had been caused by one weak moment when he'd kissed Niesha soon after his brother's death. She had consoled him, returned to being the sweet girl he'd always known and in a moment of weakness he'd taken her into his arms and kissed her. Niesha had responded but then his sense of duty had reared up like an angry stallion. He'd held her back from him and the smile on her face had told him it hadn't been about any kind of desire for him; she'd been playing with him, seeing just how far he'd go against his sense of duty.

That kiss with Niesha had been nothing like the kisses he and Tiffany had shared either here in his palace or in Paris. Those kisses had been full of genuine desire and hot passion, not at all like the kiss that had proved beyond doubt just how scheming Niesha was and that he'd had a lucky escape.

'No, there isn't any history other than having been promised to one another by our respective families.' It was pointless to enlarge on a kiss that had meant nothing, a kiss that should never have happened. He'd been at his lowest point and she'd used that to her advantage, suddenly seeing him as much more than a spare heir, a way to raise her own star.

'So you don't love her?'

'Love is not a sentiment I have any need of, Tiffany. It is what weakens a man, takes his focus off life. My brother loved his wife.' He cut the word off before he could say any more; her shocked expression left him in no doubt that, despite her claims as they'd talked at Damian's wedding, she wanted love and happy ever afters. He'd have to dispel that notion. 'Before I became the ruler of Shamsumara I put all my time and energy into my business. Women were just a pleasant distraction—and will remain so.'

'What was your business?'

He looked at her for a moment, not able to work out if his change of topic, his harsh remark that implied she was nothing more than a distraction, had been warning enough to her that she shouldn't expect any kind of love or affection from him. Her question showed him she could play the game of evasion every bit as well as him.

'You said you were the younger son who was free to build his own business.'

'I run a civil engineering company. Or rather it is currently in the capable hands of my newly appointed CEO.'

'Sounds impressive.'

'That discussion is for another day. It's getting late,' he said softly, and again the need to kiss her, to hold her close, rushed over him. He needed to send her away before he gave into the urge and gave her the wrong idea about them and their marriage. 'I will bid you goodnight.'

## CHAPTER NINE

FOR THE LAST two weeks, Tiffany had absorbed herself in the work she was expected to do while living in Shamsumara as Jafar's Queen, desperate to push aside her ever deepening feelings for a man who just saw her as a convenient bride. On the night she and Jafar had talked after the feast of gifts, he'd made it perfectly clear love was not an emotion he wanted in his life. Lust and desire were all he needed, which was exactly what Niesha had alluded to.

Since that night, Jafar had been noticeable by his absence in her new daily routine, but the process of helping women who were struggling to bring up children alone, for whatever reason, made her feel closer to Bethany. She'd talked on the phone, even had video calls, but she missed her and little Kelly terribly. Maybe she was much more homesick than she'd anticipated. It would certainly explain how emotional she'd become over the last few days.

She missed Jafar and it was more than missing the intimacy of the sex they'd shared. She missed him, missed talking with him, laughing with him. She missed the man he became when he let his guard drop in the privacy of their suite, missed him so much it made her heart ache.

She'd fallen for him. It was far more than attraction, deeper than desire. It was love. She'd fallen in love with a man who openly confessed to, not only being unable to love, but not wanting love in his life. It was an emotion he scorned.

Why had she allowed herself to fall for him, to get emotionally close to him? It was this increasing emotion, the deepening of her love, which had made her insist she slept alone from now on. The sooner she cut the tie of attraction between them, the better. She didn't mean anything to him and it would be unwise to get more involved. The only thing that mattered was the deal they'd struck.

Even the charity work she'd chosen to do while in Shamsumara didn't matter to Jafar and he had warned her about becoming too involved with those she was helping. It was almost a double standard when he'd given her the gift of a beautiful dog, which now lay at the side of her bed, waiting for her to start the day. Apart from Leah's presence, she had been alone in this bedroom since she'd rashly declared a desire to sleep alone. For two weeks her body had longed for the pleasure that Jafar's could give, as if they were made to be as one. Two whole weeks without him. Two whole weeks of torture.

A sinking realisation slipped over her and with a gasp she sat up, frantically running dates through her mind, but each time she came to the same shocking conclusion. She was late. She covered her face with her hands, beating back the tears that threatened. Was that why her emotions were all over the place?

She was pregnant.

She was pregnant with the child of a man who'd openly admitted he had no intention of ever being a father and had gone to extreme lengths to ensure he retained the kingdom he'd inherited from his late brother. He'd made sure he had the heir he required to safeguard that kingdom without the need to become a father himself, then he had hired her as his bride, negating the need to commit himself long-term to marriage.

She thought of all she'd learnt about him the night they'd talked openly, the night she'd fallen a little more in love with the man who hid behind the tough exterior of control. He'd never allowed her that close again, never let her see his guard down since that night. He had already distanced himself from the bride he'd hired, the bride he wanted to leave Shamsumara once they had been married for three months.

Could it be possible that she now carried his child? His heir?

Then the full horror of the situation hit her. Where did that leave her now? Alone and pregnant back in England? Forced to stay here with a man who'd never intended their marriage to last beyond two years? What if he sent her away after the baby was born but insisted the baby grew up in Shamsumara? Fearful thoughts made her weak, made her unsure if she wanted to cry or scream in frustration.

What she needed to do was establish if her fears were true. She needed a pregnancy test, but how did the Queen of a desert kingdom obtain that? Could she confide in Aaleyah? As soon as that idea had come to her, she dismissed it. Sweet as she seemed, Aaleyah was loyal to Jafar and her homeland. If she told her maid, then very soon Jafar would know and right now she needed to keep her suspicions from him—until she'd decided what to do. Her mind spun, making her feel light-headed with worry.

How could she have compromised herself so easily?

*Passion, desire and growing love for Jafar.*

The answer drifted around in her increasingly dizzy head but she couldn't think about that now; she had to find out if she was expecting Jafar's child.

Beyond the archway to her room, she heard the

doors to their suite burst open and guilt rushed through her at the secret she'd just realised as she heard Jafar call out her name. He never did that. Panic rushed over her. Did he know? Was there some way he'd found out already? She leapt from the bed and grabbed the silk wrap just as he strode into the room, his handsome face as dark as thunderclouds.

'What's wrong?'

'My sister has fallen.'

'Fallen?' She struggled to piece the information together, her mind still splintered after acknowledging that she was almost definitely carrying his child. She could barely process her own news, but this just scrambled her mind further.

'Down the palace steps.' He snapped the words at her as he flung off his white robes of office and put on darker ones, more suitable for an everyday man. Already he was preparing to go to her, worried about his heir.

'What about the baby?' Tiffany asked tentatively, resisting the urge to place her palm against her stomach. If the palace steps were anything like those here, it would have been a bad fall.

'That is exactly what I intend to find out. The message didn't go into detail before the signal failed.' He looked directly at her and she sensed his fear, knowing it must be bringing back memories of losing his brother. 'I must go now.'

He strode across the room to look out at the small private garden and the pale cream walls of the palace, agitation in every step, but he couldn't look at her. If he went to his sister it would give her the opportunity to find the answer to her own problems. 'Of course, you must.'

Tiffany's heart thudded. She, of course, felt for Jafar's sister, and for what she must be going through, but she also worried for what this might mean for her own situation. If his sister lost the baby, then what would become of her, of the three-month deal she'd made with Jafar? Worse than that, if she was pregnant would he allow her to leave? She had to keep her newfound secret from him. Certainly until they knew the fate of his sister and her baby.

'I need to go.' For a moment she thought she saw regret in his eyes as he looked at her. His shoulders loosened, as if he could no longer carry the weight of his kingdom, or the duties he'd inherited. A pang of sympathy rushed through her and she involuntarily moved towards him. It was that action, that hint of thought for him, that had the barriers rushing back up, until he stood tall before her, beautifully commanding and incredibly powerful. 'I must see for myself that my sister and her child are well.'

'Then go.' Her new secret burned inside her as she spoke, as did the guilt of hatching a plan to find a way to know for certain if she was carrying his child. The unspoken meaning to his words burned in her mind.

*He must have an heir.*

He adjusted his robe and picked up his headdress. 'I will return once I am satisfied my heir is safe.'

Those words ploughed into her, confirming she was right to fear his reaction if he discovered she was pregnant. How could she have been so stupid, so foolish? This wasn't an ordinary man, leading an ordinary life. This was a powerful desert sheikh who put duty to his kingdom above even his own needs—and his kingdom needed an heir.

Attack was her instant defence against that fear. 'Is that all you can think about? Satisfying yourself that your heir is safe? What about your sister? Do you not care for her?'

Anger filled his eyes as he put on his headdress and moved towards her, his voice low and threatening. 'The safety of my heir is something you should also be worried about, Tiffany. If my sister loses this baby, our marriage cannot be ended.'

The harshness he'd used as he'd said her name chased away memories of the soft, seductive way he'd said it as they'd made love on their wedding night. Then it had been a caress—a seductive caress. Now it was full of undisguised threat.

'Why?' She stood her ground even though she was seriously underdressed in only the flimsy gold silk dressing gown.

He looked at her, but his eyes didn't soften as

they slipped down her body and she folded her arms around her, needing a shield from his cold scrutiny. 'You signed a contract to stay in Shamsumara for three months or until my heir was born.'

'But that was because you knew your sister would give you the heir you needed.' She tried to defend herself, tried to remember exactly what had been in the contract but the waves of nausea were becoming ever stronger.

'The contract stated clearly that you would remain here, as my wife, my Queen, until my sister gave birth to my heir, but for a minimum of three months to validate the marriage in the eyes of my people.'

She frowned at him, her emotion-muddled mind not able to clearly follow. 'But what if the worst happens? What if she loses her baby?'

'You are my wife and, if the worst happens for my sister, you will be the only thing standing between Simdan and his challenge to my leadership of the kingdom. I cannot allow you to expose our deal by leaving—not until my sister is safely delivered of my heir.'

'And if she doesn't want more children?' Tiffany's mouth was almost too dry to speak. She needed to sit down but refused to show any kind of weakness to Jafar.

'My sister will have more children. She is a queen in her own right and needs to produce heirs for her husband's kingdom.' The calm, matter-of-fact words only intensified the heavy ache in Tiffany's heart.

'But that could take a year—or more.'

Jafar moved towards her, his voice becoming gentle, as if the panic of the news he'd just received had subsided into nothing, as if it was just the two of them once again. 'Unless our wedding night has been blessed with a child.'

Tiffany gasped. Did he know? Was this all pretence to force her to admit the truth? She hesitated a moment before speaking. 'Thankfully I am not pregnant.' She hurled the unwise words at him and stood glaring, hurt slashing into the tenderness she'd been carrying in her heart for him since he'd claimed her as his wife, become her first lover, then lowered his guard and showed her the true Jafar.

Was it just the shadows cast by the morning sunlight or was there disappointment in his eyes? She closed her eyes against the fanciful notion as the dizziness threatened once more, making her mind sway like the dancers at their celebration feast. The reality of his words made her body weaken. She was trapped. If his sister lost her baby her fate was sealed; whether she admitted that she might be carrying his child or not, she could no longer leave. Her head spun with the seriousness of her situation and the knowledge she couldn't keep her secret from him for ever.

'Tiffany?' Concern filled his voice and she looked at Jafar as his handsome face blurred, her ability to focus slipping away, then nothing but blissfully silent darkness.

Jafar called out for Aaleyah as Tiffany slipped to the floor in front of him. Her face was pale as he scooped her into his arms and carried her to the large bed they'd shared with much passion on their wedding night, three weeks ago. Just as then, desire and lust forged through him as he touched her. He held her close against his body, painfully aware of the flimsy silk doing very little to conceal the fullness of her breasts.

Beside him Leah whimpered and nuzzled Tiffany's hand as he laid Tiffany on the bed. What was the matter with her? He'd been guilty of neglecting her for the two weeks since they'd resumed normal life, but it had been the only way to stop himself from wanting her. Was she now so homesick she didn't eat? Was that why she'd fainted so spectacularly?

*It was your threat to force her to stay.*

His conscience screamed the answer to his question and it seemed to echo around the velvety silence of the room. 'I'm so sorry, Tiffany, for dragging you into my battles. I never wanted to hurt you.'

He stroked her hair as he sat on the edge of the bed next to her, the need to care for and protect her overwhelmingly strong. If he had a normal life, if he was able to want normal things, then he would want Tiffany. He'd want her to remain in his life, to care for her and maybe he might even be able to let go of his past and allow love into his heart.

*You don't have a normal life.*

Aaleyah rushed to the bedside, thankfully cutting off his unthinkable train of thought, and he looked up at her, a sensation of total helplessness almost suffocating him. Tiffany and his sister. The two women he cared deeply about and they were both in need of his presence. He refused to analyse that thought right now. The fact that he considered Tiffany a woman he cared about was almost too much on top of the events of this morning.

'What is the matter with her?' Jafar demanded of his wife's maid.

A smile slipped to Aaleyah's lips. Not at all the reaction he had anticipated. Not at all the sense of panic and loss of control that had him in its grip. 'I have suspected for a few days, even perhaps before Her Majesty.'

'Suspected what, damn it?' Jafar snapped as he sat beside Tiffany's limp body. He didn't want guessing games. He wanted to make things right for Tiffany, make her smile and laugh as she had done during their week alone. Despite everything he'd promised himself, he cared for her—deeply. 'Is she ill? Is it the heat?'

'You are to be a father, sire.'

Jafar froze as the maid's words sank in and he looked down at Tiffany as she groaned softly and stirred. His beautiful wife, the woman who'd made him think happiness could be possible, was pregnant? He was going to be a father? Elation poured through him but as he looked again at Aaleyah, who still seemed remarkably unconcerned for her mistress, all he could hear was Tiffany's words before she'd collapsed ringing in his mind. 'Are you sure?'

'Yes, sire. I have been watching for signs that your bride is with child. That is my job.' The maid looked satisfied with the explanation for her mistress passing out. He, however, felt only concern. He'd never wanted Tiffany to suffer. That had never been part of his deal.

Tiffany stirred once more, this time struggling to sit up. Cold hardness filled him, pushing away the gentle affection and concern of moments ago. Tiffany had lied. His pregnant wife had told him she wasn't carrying his child—only a few moments ago. What could she possibly hope to gain from keeping such news from him? Her freedom?

'Leave us.' He snapped the command at the maid without taking his eyes from the beauty of Tiffany's treacherous face, unable to deal with the revelations of the last few minutes and certainly not with the emotions that had surged through him for his Tiffany. He adopted the only stance he knew and sat rigid with anger on the bed beside her as Aaleyah called to the dog and left the room. For the first time in two weeks he and Tiffany were alone. Totally alone.

Jafar's breath was deep and hard as Tiffany looked up at him and he reeled in the shock of all that had just happened. Less than an hour ago, he'd learnt his sister's child, his planned heir, was in danger. Now this. *His* child had been conceived with great passion during the hottest night of sex he'd ever had. His hired bride, the woman he'd brought to his country as a temporary measure, carried his child. His heir.

'You lied.' Guilt slashed at him as he inwardly cursed his position, the duty his brother had left him. Since their wedding night he'd wished for more, wished it hadn't been part of a deal, but his duty meant that could never be possible.

Sparks of angry fire leapt from her eyes as she looked directly into his, refusing to break eye contact. The vulnerability of moments ago, when she'd lain pale and asleep on the bed, had gone, chasing away those unfamiliar gentle feelings for her. This was a woman intent on fighting her corner.

Tiffany fought to keep her breathing calm, to keep looking into the wildness of her husband's eyes. They had once held nothing but desire and passion for her; now they were hard, glittering with anger.

'You lied to me.' The glacial words cooled the air around them until she visibly shivered as Jafar spoke again.

She knew what he was talking about. She had no idea how, but he knew she was almost certainly pregnant. From the foggy recesses of her mind she recalled Aaleyah's voice, coming through the darkness that had claimed her, how she'd calmly told Jafar he was to be a father. How did her maid know before she did?

Shame burned over her. She was so innocent, so unaware of sex she hadn't even considered the need for protection on their wedding night. She'd just been swept away with the fantasy of the magical room, lit by lanterns. Transported on the warm desert wind that had come in through the archways, entwining with the soft music and totally seducing her. She'd been a victim of her own dreams, dreams of love and happiness she'd long ago thought buried. She'd been completely under his spell.

Was that why Lilly had left such an obscure present? To remind her not to get carried away with things that could never be, as well as protect her from the consequences of the attraction she'd admitted she had for Jafar?

'Why, Tiffany?' Jafar glared at her, his eyes sparking with anger in a way that would put a priceless gem to shame.

'I did not lie,' she snapped at Jafar, her emotions running high, making her ever more vulnerable to this man, even in his current angry mood.

'You clearly told me that you were not expecting my child. *"Thankfully I am not pregnant."* Those were your exact words, yet just moments later you are on the floor at my feet. Aaleyah informed me she has suspected for several days. How long have you known?'

The sharpness of the accusation in his voice cut deep into her. She hadn't kept anything from him. 'I don't know for sure. It was only this morning I realised it was possible.'

'It's been possible since our wedding night, Tiffany.'

Was he trying to make her look stupid? 'I can

hardly go to the local pharmacy and buy a pregnancy test, can I?'

She swung her legs from the bed, needing to get away from him, away from the pain and hurt of his obvious disgust at the idea of being, not only a father, but the father of her child. As soon as she stood up she wished she hadn't as the room spun once more.

She put her hand to her head, pressing her fingers to her temple, wishing she didn't feel so weak, so at this man's mercy. She heard the bed move as she stood, her body sensing his behind her, and she closed her eyes as her body begged for his touch.

'Hadn't you better go?' She was desperate to deflect the attention from herself. 'Your sister needs you.'

'As do you—and my child.'

She turned to face him. 'I am not sure, Jafar, that I am pregnant, despite what Aaleyah said.'

'I would believe the wise ways of a woman such as Aaleyah over a doctor any day.' His voice had become gentle, his eyes softening, and all that she'd been trying to hide from herself burst back into the open. She loved this man and had done from the day she'd become his wife—maybe sooner if she was really honest with herself.

He touched the backs of his fingers over her cheeks and she began to melt, her promise to never let him touch her again slipping by the wayside. This was why it was dangerous to be alone with him. She couldn't trust herself. 'I will arrange for a doctor to visit to confirm if you are pregnant.'

'And if I am?' Even to her, the words were a tremulous whisper that gave away so much. Panic rushed through her like a tidal wave, sweeping away to softer emotions she'd foolishly allowed back into her heart. It changed everything—for both of them, putting them in a situation neither had ever wanted.

He trailed the backs of his fingers down her face, her throat, over the exposed skin of her chest, down between her breasts and then placed his palm against her stomach. She didn't move. Couldn't move. Her breath became fast and shallow as his gaze pierced into her, seemingly reading every thought in her mind.

'If you are pregnant, I will do everything in my power to convince you to remain in Shamsumara as my wife and Queen.'

# CHAPTER TEN

JAFAR PACED THE room beyond the bedroom where the doctor he'd summoned was attending his wife. There it was again. He'd never wanted to think of Tiffany as his wife. She'd always only ever been his bride—his hired bride, but somehow in his thoughts she'd become his wife.

Firm footsteps alerted him to the doctor and he turned expectantly to face him, realising with a jolt he wanted Aaleyah's diagnosis of Tiffany's fainting to be true. He wanted his wife to be expecting his child. The thought slammed into him like a sandstorm, taking his breath away. How had everything he'd ever wanted changed so much? He'd never wanted to father a child, never wanted to inflict that same censure he'd received on his child.

'Her Highness is indeed expecting. Congratulations, Your Highness.' The doctor's words seemed to come from far away, reaching him as if on the wings of his falcon. If he never wanted a child, why did this news fill him with such elation?

He thanked the older man and returned to his bedchamber to see that Tiffany was now up and dressed in a deep blue silk dress, adorned with diamonds. She looked stunning and his chest tightened.

As if sensing her presence wouldn't be needed, Aaleyah slipped discreetly away, but Leah remained lying on the cool marble floor close to her mistress. Tiffany turned and looked at him. He saw her throat move delicately as she swallowed, giving away her nerves.

Did she fear the situation they were now in as parents-to-be? Was it possible she didn't want his child? He moved towards her, her eyes watchful, mirroring all the doubt, all the questions that were racing through his mind.

'It is confirmed.' His voice was hard with controlled anger, the only way he knew how to deal with situations that evoked deep emotions within him that he didn't want. 'You carry the heir of Shamsumara.'

'And what exactly do you propose to do about that?' The starkness of that question was in sharp contrast to the soft image she created in a blue gown. Her long brown hair loose, framing her face, accentuating her freckles. He ignored the effect she had on him, pushed it savagely away. Instead he drew on the curtness of her words, the blame laced within them, blame that lay firmly at his feet.

'You are my legal wife. There is nothing to be done.'

'I am your hired bride. You paid me to come here for three months. Surely that goes against one of your traditions. There must be a way out of this.'

'The night we came to this very bedchamber after our wedding you were a virgin, untouched by any man, and in taking that from you I broke one of the most sacred beliefs of my country.' He'd spent many hours dwelling on this fact. He'd married a virgin bride—unknowingly, but that changed nothing. Not when he'd allowed desire to consume him so intensely that he'd refused to adhere to the sacred tradition of the rules of Shamsumara, that a virgin bride could never be cast aside.

'There are so many beliefs, so many traditions. We must have broken most of them just by signing the contract.'

'That is true, but even though it wasn't a real marriage I took something that was not rightfully mine to take.' He moved closer to her and she looked up at him, her eyes searching his. 'We could have lived with that secret, but now that you are carrying my child, it is very different.'

She pushed her way past him, exasperation in every move she made, and he watched, a helpless sensation rushing over him. All he wanted to do was take away her pain, soothe her troubled mind.

'It must have been that stupid flower.' She flopped down to sit on the bed, her hands covering her face in a gesture of despair.

Jafar had that sensation tight around his chest again and sat down next to her, pulling her hand gently from her face. 'The flower is nothing more than a tradition. I hold myself totally responsible for the situation we are in now. I should have taken care of contraception—especially when you told me you were a virgin.'

Her lips lifted into a sad smile. 'It's not all your fault. I wanted that night with you. I'm as much to blame.'

'No.' He could never allow her to take any blame. She might have driven him mad with desire, seduced him with her soft words of wanting one night, but she was inexperienced, he was not.

'I just wish I had opened Lilly's gift sooner.' The regret and turmoil in her voice dragged his guilt further out into the open.

'But you didn't.' He laid his hand over hers, shocked to feel how cool it was and eager to take away the blame she was pouring over herself. 'Have you thought that fate has conspired to bring us together, to give us the baby that was created that night with such passion?'

She blushed and that familiar rush of lust hurtled through him. Would he ever stop wanting this woman? 'It wasn't fate, Jafar. It was my innocence—or maybe ignorance.'

He cupped her face in his hands, forcing her to look at him. 'I am honoured to have been the man you chose to be your first.'

She pulled away from him. 'I should never have done that. I don't know what happened to me. Maybe it was the total fantasy of being in a desert kingdom, maybe I was trying to live the fairy tale. I'd longed for the perfect fairy-tale wedding and then here I was, with a man like you—on my wedding night.'

'What are your true thoughts on marriage?' He had to ask, had to know. He hadn't told her yet that there was almost no way out of their marriage now that she carried his child and most certainly wouldn't be if anything happened to his sister's baby. He pressed that thought away, not daring to tempt fate by thinking it any more. His sister and her baby would be fine; they had to be.

'My parents married because my mother fell

pregnant with Bethany. Five years later I arrived but by then the marriage was already in trouble. I always thought I was a last-ditch attempt at making it work but love had turned sour and I don't remember any affection between my parents. It was a relief when they finally split up and later divorced.'

'It just proves there is no such thing as true love or one that lasts a lifetime. What brings a man and woman together is more basic than that.'

Her brows furrowed together and the look of sadness in her eyes was almost unbearable. 'Sex. It's all about sex. I know. I had several boyfriends but never let them get close—in any way. I was searching for the impossible dream and being here with you on our wedding night was it, but I was wrong. I guess I just got carried away with the fantasy when really it was just sex.'

Was she too hiding from her feelings towards him? 'It was more than just sex. It was desire. Hot passion.'

Tiffany jumped up as if she couldn't bear being near him. 'Whatever it was, it was wrong. It should never have happened. I just hope everything is all right with your sister and her baby. Then I can leave here and forget all this ever happened.'

'Leave?'

'Yes, leave, Jafar. I have to go back to my life.'

'And what of my child?'

'It's a child you don't want. You made that very clear and I will never bother you, never darken your door and demand anything from you emotionally or financially, you don't have to worry about that, but I am leaving.'

'I have a duty to my child, one that I intend to take very seriously.' He stood up and inhaled deeply, instilling control back into him, blocking out the way he felt towards this woman.

'I don't want my baby to grow up as I did, Jafar.' She looked at him, imploring him to understand, and he did, but he didn't want her to leave, not now she carried his baby.

'I will never allow that.' His passionate response shocked him to the core. Already he was protective over the child their night of passion had created. It was far deeper than the need to protect his heir in a way he couldn't yet understand. He needed time and space to deal with all he'd just discovered and the best way to get that was to go and see his sister. 'I must go and see my sister. See for myself what has happened. You will remain here with Aaleyah until I return and only then will we discuss our marriage.'

Jafar's threat had remained in the charged atmosphere of their suite long after the doctor had left, having declared the new Queen to be with child. Tiffany had been relieved when Jafar had told her he had to go to his sister, but that had been short-lived as he had called in Aaleyah, instructing her to remain with his wife every moment of the day and night while he was away.

Aaleyah had done exactly as instructed and had remained with Tiffany throughout the day and night while Jafar had gone to see his sister. Now they had received word of his imminent return and her maid had left her alone to prepare yet another fragrant bath for her, although Tiffany secretly wondered if it wasn't more for her ruler. The notion of that old-fashioned view still didn't detract from the pleasure of the scented baths and all the pampering that went with it.

Tiffany slipped out of one of the exquisite silk dresses she'd found waiting for her on arrival in Shamsumara and pulled on a white cotton dressing gown, preferring it to the gold silk she'd worn on her first morning of marriage. That seemed far too decadent now.

She tied the belt at her waist, looking forward to soaking in the deep warm waters of the bath. It would soothe not only her troubled mind, but her weakened body. She looked in the mirror and rested her hands on her stomach, hardly able to believe she was pregnant with Jafar's child, much less the way he'd calmly told her he would do anything to convince her to stay.

Behind her she heard movement from the arch that led onto the small plant-filled garden set aside for her use alone. By day it was a cool shady place, a haven from the heat of the sun. By night it was lit by lanterns near the archway, but shrouded in darkness beyond.

'Jafar?' His name slipped from her lips even though she knew he hadn't ever used this way into their suite. When no response came, fear slithered down her spine, but she reassured herself it must be Aaleyah. She tried not to let her imagination run riot, tried not to think of what or who could be in the darkness beyond the light from the lanterns. She was just being fanciful yet again and it had to stop.

She turned back to the mirror and pulled her long hair from the pins that held it firmly away from her face and as it tumbled down her back she looked again in the mirror. How could she ever believe Jafar, a desert ruler, could fall in love with a pale-faced English girl when there were beautiful women around him like Niesha?

She took in a deep breath as the woman who made no secret of her dislike for the English bride Jafar had returned home with forced her way back into Tiffany's thoughts. She was in no doubt that something had happened between her husband and Niesha, although she knew enough of her husband's view of honour to know it would not be happening now that they were both married.

The rustling of leaves from the garden made her turn once again. 'Who's there?'

She waited, holding her breath, but nothing. Slowly she walked towards the arch, stepping out beyond the soft yellow light of the lanterns into the darkness of the garden. Jafar wouldn't torment her like this, wouldn't send fear through her. She placed her hand on the cool marble of the arch and leant into the darkness, about to ask again.

The hand that caught her face, pressing hard over her lips as the assailant stood behind her, was hard and calloused, a large ring pressing into her cheek. She tried to scream but the hand smothered her mouth.

'Screaming will get you nowhere, Your Royal Highness.' Simdan. She'd recognise that deep and menacing voice anywhere.

She stopped struggling and stood, hating the

smell of his hand on her face, but knowing that to show fear would be the worst thing possible with this man. She resisted the urge to struggle as he pushed her into the garden, into the darkness as menacing as the man who held his hand over her mouth. He forced her through a gateway and into a tunnel that was so black she had no idea where they were, then she saw stars high in the night sky as they emerged into the desert beyond the palace walls.

Was he kidnapping her?

'I have brought you here to strike a deal with you,' Simdan said, putting his face close to hers. 'And we both know how much you like to make deals.'

'I think you should let me go.' Tiffany forced the words from her, adamant this horrible man wouldn't know just how terrified she was.

He moved towards her and she backed up against the wall, realising very quickly how wrong that was. 'Do you indeed?'

'Yes, Jafar will return any moment now.'

'How can you be so sure when he has gone to

the mother of his heir.' The laugh that erupted from Simdan turned Tiffany's stomach over and she felt sick.

'What do you want?'

'To buy you just as easily as my cousin did.' He laughed again. A cold sound that made her heart thud with fear as adrenalin raced around her. 'I will pay you three times what he did—if you leave now.'

'If I go anywhere it will not be because you have paid me.' The reply rushed from her before she'd even thought if it was wise. As far as she was concerned she would be leaving because she wanted to, not because either of the desert Kings had paid her to do so.

'If you stay, Your Royal Highness, I will expose your deal to the people of Shamsumara. I wonder how they will view their new Queen then. A hired bride. A bought woman.'

She knew full well it was nothing to do with how the people thought of her, it was how they viewed their ruler. Jafar would lose their support and, without an heir, Simdan could make his claim to be ruler of the kingdom. She couldn't stand by and allow the man she'd fallen in love with, the man whose child she now carried, be so completely destroyed.

Jafar returned to his marital suite to find it empty. Something was wrong. He could feel it on the warm breeze, sense it deep within him as if a connection had long ago been forged with Tiffany, a connection he'd fought hard against. His sister was well and her pregnancy was unthreatened and all he wanted to do was tell Tiffany he wanted her, wanted his child, that he wanted to try and fulfil her dreams.

Aaleyah entered the suite and looked at Jafar. 'Where is Her Highness?'

'I assumed you were following orders and that you hadn't left her alone?' He'd known Simdan would try something to discredit his and Tiffany's marriage, but had never expected him to stoop so low and take advantage of his sister's fall and kidnap Tiffany.

If she had left the suite by the main doors, the

guards he'd thankfully had the foresight to place there would have seen her. There was only one other way out of the palace. The secret tunnel.

Without a moment to lose Jafar rushed through the garden, the trickle of the water from the fountain now an ominous sound. He pushed open the wooden door in the archway with ease and then stepped into the tunnel. Tiffany's scent that he knew so well lingered like a trail in the darkness.

How could he have put her at such risk? How could he have done this to the woman he loved?

He stopped in the tunnel. The echo of that thought made all the more powerful in the heavy darkness. He loved Tiffany. The bride he'd hired had found her way past every barrier he'd put around his heart. She'd unlocked the door to emotions he'd vowed never to succumb to.

He swore savagely in his native language as he strode on through the darkness, pausing when he heard Simdan's voice beyond the opening to the desert, low and threatening—and speaking in English, confirming his suspicions.

'What else did Jafar get for his money?' The

suggestive snarl that followed this remark turned Jafar to ice and he gritted his teeth against the building hatred for his cousin. 'Did he get this?'

Jafar had no idea what *this* was, but from the protesting gasps Tiffany made he could well guess and, like a panther that had been stalking its prey, waiting for the opportune moment, he stealthily moved out of the darkness, finally ready to confront his enemy.

'Take your hands off her.' Jafar's hard voice filled the silence of the night and Tiffany's relief was intense.

Simdan backed away, his hands held up, proving he had no intention of touching her again. Revulsion filled her as he leered at her. 'I was only taking from you what you took from me.' He turned his attention back to Jafar. 'You kissed Niesha. You couldn't take it that she'd chosen me instead of you. You tried to seduce her, tried to break our union apart.'

'What I took from Niesha was given gladly,' Jafar fired back at his cousin, and Tiffany's heart broke, right there in front of these warring men. The man she loved didn't love her and never would. He was still in love with the woman his family had planned for him to marry, the woman who had married his cousin. Now the intense hatred between them made sense.

Simdan's eyes narrowed with aggression as he looked from her to Jafar, the darkness of the night unable to conceal the pure venom in them.

'What you intend to take from my wife, however, is not given willingly. My wife is not yours for the taking.' Jafar squared up to his adversary. 'Just as my kingdom is not. Go back to your wife and child, Simdan. Focus on your own kingdom.'

Guards burst out of the tunnel, grabbed Simdan, and Tiffany shrank back against the palace walls. Jafar gave instructions and, by the light of the half-moon and the stars, the foreign words, hard and unyielding, filling the night air, Tiffany almost fell to the sand. In silence she watched Simdan being taken away.

Shock at what had just happened numbed her and she barely felt Jafar's touch as he pulled her against him, but his warmth helped to soothe her panic as it gently thawed her. It did little for the pain in her heart knowing he didn't really want her in his life, that the woman he wanted was now married to his cousin.

She pulled back from Jafar, looking up at him as the cool night breeze of the desert played with her hair. 'Your sister?'

In the darkness she could feel his relief. 'She and the baby are well.'

There was only one more thing she needed to know and she had to ask him now. 'Did you kiss Niesha?'

'I'm not proud of it, but, yes, I did.'

'Did she kiss you too?' His hard words to his cousin replayed in her mind. *What I took from Niesha was given gladly.*

Tiffany knew right there, as the stars sparkled in the night sky, that she couldn't stay with Jafar. She was a fool to think she could see their deal through to the end, salvage his reputation, but she'd be even more of a fool to stay with a man who didn't want her, much less love her.

Now that she knew she was pregnant she had to leave. There was no way she wanted her child to grow up witnessing the kind of fierce rows she'd seen between parents who hadn't wanted to be together. There might well be passion between her and Jafar now, but passion never lasted, not with a man like her husband. He'd soon find another woman more desirable, then another.

'I'm leaving.' She turned with her chin held high and marched as best she could in the sand back towards the tunnel. She didn't want to go into the darkness again, but she wanted to stay out here with Jafar even less. She couldn't stand the pain of even being near him knowing there wasn't any hope of a future for her and her child with this man, despite his bold proclamations of duty and honour.

'What do you mean you are leaving?' Jafar caught her arm and pulled her round to face him.

'I'm leaving Shamsumara right now.'

'It's the middle of the night and you are not in a fit state to travel,' Jafar declared, and the lack of trying to dissuade her from leaving only made her certain it was the right thing to do.

'There is nothing wrong with me.'

'You are pregnant.'

'And we both know that was not part of our deal, not what you wanted at all.' She stood and stared at him, challenging him to say otherwise, daring him to break his terms.

'It wasn't, no.'

'Now that your sister is well and the baby too, I think it's best if I return to England.'

He looked at her without saying a word, shadows from the palace walls falling over his face rendering it as unreadable as ever. His silence, his hesitancy confirmed she was doing the right thing. He didn't want her or his baby.

'At least wait until the morning. I will arrange for my plane to be on standby and if returning to England is still what you want I will not stop you, but don't leave now. Not after what has just happened.'

Agonising pain slashed at her heart. He wasn't prepared to fight for her or even his child. Sadness percolated through her as she accepted he'd never love her. 'I won't change my mind, Jafar. I am leaving.'

# CHAPTER ELEVEN

THE NEXT MORNING Tiffany woke early with a sense of foreboding, after a restless night that had seen her tossing and turning. Aaleyah had slept in one of the suite's other rooms for a second night and Tiffany couldn't decide if she was being guarded or protected. Or even worse, if it was the child she now carried that was being watched over.

With her mind still restless she sat up in the large bed she'd slept alone in. Last night, after the incident with Simdan, she'd told Jafar she was leaving and he hadn't even tried to persuade her to stay. He'd ordered Aaleyah to remain a second night in her company because he hadn't cared enough for her to do so himself.

These thoughts had whirred in her mind all night and as she'd finally given up on sleep she had come to her decision. She had to leave Jafar, leave Shamsumara and end this sham of a marriage. Not for his sake, or hers, but for the life they'd created. A baby he had admitted to never wanting.

All she could think about now was returning to England and starting a new life, where she could prepare for motherhood alone. It was ironic that she now faced this prospect when she'd come here to help Bethany do the same. Now she too was destined to be a single mother.

She ran her fingers through her hair, feeling more dishevelled than ever, but there was no way she was going to allow Jafar to see her like this. She would leave the palace full of pride with her head held high. With that thought in mind she showered and dressed in one of her own summer dresses, shunning the vast array of colourful silks Jafar had filled her closet with.

Aaleyah entered the room and stopped, the smile of greeting she always had missing from her face. 'A car is ready to transfer you to the plane.'

'Thank you, Aaleyah. There is one further

thing I need you to do.' She looked at the maid, forcing hardness into her heart, trying to block out the pain of everything from saying goodbye to her beautiful dog, to walking out on the man she loved.

*He will never love you.*

Words that had filled her mind during the long wakeful hours of last night sounded once more. 'I need you to take care of Leah. As much as I would like to take her, I can't.'

'As you wish.' Aaleyah patted her leg and Leah trotted over to her. Neither of them seemed worried that she was leaving and it just convinced her all the more she was doing the right thing. Pregnant or not, she couldn't stay here any longer. Not when the man she loved would never love her in return.

She wanted to ask where Jafar was, wanted to know if he was going to see her before she went. He might not want her as his wife any longer, might not want to acknowledge her child as his heir, but he was still the father of her child created during a night of passion. Surely that counted for something? Pride stopped her from saying anything. His message was more than clear.

He didn't want her in his life and she wouldn't beg.

'Good, then I'm ready to leave.' Tiffany picked up the one small bag of her possessions and walked out of the suite that held such bittersweet memories for her. She bit down hard against the sadness and the tears that threatened. Crying seemed to be her default setting at the moment, but she wouldn't give in to that need. Not now. Not until she was high above the desert and well on her way back to England.

Without a backward glance she left the luxurious Royal Suite and with head held high made her way to the waiting car.

A large black SUV waited in the shade of the palace entrance, the finality of its presence taking her breath away. Jafar really did want her gone. What had she expected? That he would be here waiting to stop her, begging her not to leave, declaring undying love for her? That was the stuff of fairy tales with happy endings. That was the fantasy she knew would never happen. Jafar's absence as she walked out of his life was reality. This was the end of their deal, the end of their marriage and the start of her new life.

She'd arrived in Shamsumara a virgin and had fallen in love with the man she'd been hired to marry. She had lost her virginity to him in a night of such intense pleasure it still made heat curl deep within her to think about it and she now carried that man's child. Her life would never be the same again, but she was determined that if that child was a son she would show him so much love and affection he would never hurt a woman as Jafar had hurt her.

Her bag was taken from her by one of the palace servants, jolting her thoughts back to the painful moment of walking away. She stood proud and tall, the wind whipping the long skirt of her dress around, and waited as the back door of the SUV was opened for her. She climbed in, feeling more alone than she'd ever felt, despite the driver, dressed in white robes and a headdress, who sat patiently and wordlessly waiting. The door shut with a soft clunk, the engine started and the vehicle moved away from the palace. She wouldn't look back, didn't want to know if somewhere Jafar was watching her leave.

She didn't want to look at the desert either. Instead she rested her head back against the soft leather seats of the SUV and closed her eyes. Soon this would all be over and she allowed the motion of the vehicle to soothe her, allowed it to lull her briefly to sleep.

She woke with a start when the SUV stopped and looked out through the darkened windows. All she could see was desert, but the driver got out and she assumed Jafar had had his plane made ready at a different airfield. Maybe he didn't want her seen leaving, didn't want to make his wife's departure public knowledge yet, which would surely happen at the bustle of the one they'd landed at almost five weeks ago. So much had happened since then. Had it really only been six weeks since she'd agreed to Jafar's deal?

Her door opened and the driver, swathed in white robes and a white headdress, which he wore wrapped around his face, stood back. He averted his gaze as she stepped out into the rising heat of the morning, clutching in vain at her dress to keep her legs covered. She looked around her in alarm. This wasn't an airfield. This was the middle of the desert and all she could see were several tents. There was no sign of a plane anywhere.

'Where am I?' The man merely turned and walked towards the tents, the keys of the SUV jangling noticeably in his hand. Either he didn't understand English or refused to speak to her.

Should she follow? What if this was another attempt by Simdan? She looked at the SUV behind her but of course that was useless. Even if the driver had left the keys in it she would have no idea in which direction to drive off. She was completely at the mercy of the driver—and whoever else was here, in the middle of nowhere, waiting in the tent.

She looked across at the largest of the tents, to see the driver standing next to the opening, framed by ornately carved wood. Through the opening she could see vibrant colours and soft lighting, which contrasted completely with the plain sand-coloured exterior of the fabric that rippled gently in the wind. He didn't meet her gaze, exactly what she'd come to expect from the men who served Jafar, but should she follow him, go into the tent? As the question raced through her mind at top speed he gestured her to him, then into the tent. He obviously didn't speak any English.

Tentatively she walked towards the tent, her sandals allowing the cool sand beneath the heated surface to seep in with each step she took. Her stomach knotted in fear, but the driver now stood motionless by the intricately carved wood, which gave the plain tent a majestic look. This wasn't just an ordinary tent. She was sure of that. Fear curled inside her again. Was Simdan behind this? Was Jafar right now searching for her in his palace?

She pushed the fear-driven thoughts aside and paused as she drew level with the driver but, just as before, he gestured her inside, his eyes still downcast, his headdress making it impossible to see if she recognised him as one of Jafar's servants. With nerves racing over her, she stepped onto the carpet that covered the desert sand and into the tent. The heady scent of incense filled the air, soft seductive music weaved around her. It was the ultimate desert fantasy, the kind of place she'd imagined being with Jafar, before events had destroyed all those romantic ideas.

A noise behind her made her swing round to see the driver with his back to her, closing the tent. 'I need to get to the airport,' she blurted out as panic sluiced over her once more, but he continued his task in slow methodical movements as if he hadn't heard her, let alone understood.

'I have to go,' she tried again, not able to keep the panic from her voice any more.

This time he turned to face her and for the first time looked directly at her. There was no mistaking those eyes. 'Jafar.'

'You didn't think I was going to let you walk away so easily, did you?'

Why was it every time he needed to draw on his strength of control, Tiffany always looked so utterly vulnerable or incredibly desirable? Right now her eyes were full of doubt and vulnerability as she looked at him. They became larger as he moved towards her, but her body, today dressed in a long black dress splashed with large cream flowers, was the most desirable he'd ever seen it, reminding him of how she'd looked that Sunday morning after Damian's wedding.

Then she'd filled him with hot desire and he recalled how he'd thought that if he weren't setting out a marriage contract with her he would have taken her to his suite and made love to her. Would he have wanted the same if he'd known then she had been a virgin? Would he have put such a deal to her, knowing his ability to resist the temptation she created would be hard to achieve?

'Yes.' That one word snapped with alarming confidence from her.

'Then you are very much mistaken.' He threw the hard words into the charged atmosphere inside the tent, ratcheting up the tension to unbearable levels.

'But why here?' She spread her hands wide and looked around the desert tent he often used as his escape. This was his royal hideaway and could be assembled wherever he wanted it to be. Today it was in the middle of the desert, far away from the palace and the capital city of Shamsumara and, more importantly, far away from the airfield where his plane was on standby—awaiting his further instructions. Instructions he hoped would be to stand down, but with the fierce expression of determination on his wife's beautiful face he seriously doubted that would be the case.

'Because we can be alone.' He moved closer to her, smiling as she proudly held her ground, looking as poised as any queen could. He recalled the first time he'd thought she possessed the regal qualities fit for a queen of Shamsumara and now he was in no doubt. He also knew that he wanted her as his Queen, wanted her to be the mother of the heir to his kingdom. All he could do now was hope that it wasn't too late, that she didn't despise him for all that had happened. If he'd been the loving husband he should have been he would not only have protected her from his cousin's evil attempts to take what wasn't his, he would have protected her on their wedding night.

*But then you would have no reason to make her stay.*

The words chanted in his mind as he stood watching her, trying to predict her next move.

*You would lose the woman you love.*

'But I don't want to be alone with you,' she protested defiantly. 'I want to go home—to England.'

'And so you shall—if that is what you truly want. All I ask is to spend one last night with you.' The request was audacious, but then he was a bold and courageous man. He was also a man who would do anything to get what he wanted and right now that was Tiffany.

She gasped and this time took a step back, shaking her head slowly. 'No, Jafar.'

'Nothing will happen that you don't want to happen,' he assured her, recalling how he'd said those words to her about their wedding night, the night she had asked for more, asked him to make love to her, asked him to fulfil her fantasy. That night had been about passion, but tonight, if she allowed him to show her, would be different. Tonight would be about love—his love for her.

'We both know what happened the last time you said that.' The barb hit home, but he rebuffed it.

'You told me you were a virgin. You also told me you wanted to be mine.' His voice became hoarse with the memory of that night as guilt rushed at him again, almost unbalancing him. 'That you wanted the fantasy of a night with a desert sheikh.'

She looked down, her long lashes sweeping onto her pale skin; the freckles he'd always found so endearing were more pronounced from her recent time in the sun.

'None of this is about us any more, Jafar. It's about our child.' She looked from lowered lashes at him.

'I am well aware of that.' He moved away from

her and picked up a headscarf, holding it out to her. 'Put this on. I have something I wish to show you.'

She frowned at him, but did as he asked, hiding her glorious long brown hair beneath the cream silk. 'I will show you why I come to the desert, why I have this escape route ready at all times. This way.'

He walked back out into the heat of the morning, sensing with every muscle in his body that she was following. He ducked his head and went into one of the other tents erected close to his quarters. His falcon sat patiently on its wooden perch, having been transported here ahead of them.

'My goodness,' Tiffany said from behind him as he put on the suede glove and untethered the falcon and placed her on his arm. She stretched her wings and then settled as he looked at Tiffany.

'Her name is Shae.' He ran his hand over the bird's back to calm her. 'She is excited to fly. I usually fly her much earlier in the day, but today, I wanted you here. I wanted you to see her fly.'

'What has she got to do with us? I don't understand.' She shook her head in confusion and, despite the curtness of her question, he was pleased to see she was intrigued.

'Come.' He left the tent, walking out into the openness of the desert. Then he turned to Tiffany, who was struggling to keep her dress around her legs even more than she had done at the palace. He caught a glimpse of a long slender thigh, pale and soft, and although it unleased a stab of lust he pushed it aside. 'She will now fly.'

He removed the bird's hood and she stood poised, her wings out. Then with a flurry of movement she took off, sweeping around them in the sky. He didn't take his focus off the bird. If he looked at Tiffany's body, the fabric of her dress plastered close against it by the wind, he would lose all control. This was about showing Tiffany she had her freedom, that he would set her free to fly like his falcon if that was what she wanted. He'd do it because he loved her, even though it would kill him.

'That is wonderful,' Tiffany said as she stood a little way behind him. 'To see her fly free like that.'

He smiled. That was exactly the reaction he'd hoped for. After watching the bird a while longer, he held out his arm and she returned, rewarded with the food he'd held, the protection he offered. 'And now she returns to me of her own free will.'

He looked at Tiffany. 'Tomorrow, I will do as you ask and set you free but I hope that, after tonight, you too will want to be with me and accept all I can give you.'

He wasn't yet ready to tell her that he wanted to give her his love, that he'd realised he wasn't immune to the emotion, that he'd fallen in love with her and, if he was honest with himself, it was while she was attending Damian's bride he'd done that. He'd just been too proud, too controlled and too shielded behind his defensive wall to realise it.

All he could think about was her rejection, her

need to leave him, leave Shamsumara. If she loved him, then surely she wouldn't want to do that. It was her determination to leave that silenced his words, prevented him from admitting his love.

Tiffany couldn't find anything to say to Jafar's declaration. Did he really think one more night of passion would be enough to make her change her mind, to make her stay and complete the deal she'd agreed to? One more night in this man's arms, tasting his kisses, enjoying his caress was all she wanted, but she couldn't. To do that would render her incapable of doing what had to be done—walking away.

'Tomorrow I will still feel the same,' she said, annoyed he thought he only had to bring her out here, play out her ultimate desert fantasy, in order to get her to stay a little longer. He could never give her what she wanted. He could never give her his love. He'd already admitted that to her and had coldly told her he never wished to be a father.

'Then I have much to do to ensure you change

your mind.' He put the hood back on the falcon and returned to the tent.

The dark coolness of the tent was a relief from the heat of the desert and the warm winds as Tiffany followed him back inside, watching as he settled the bird on her perch once more. His voice was soft and gentle as he spoke to Shae in his own language, each move he made full of tenderness, which took Tiffany's mind hurtling back to those blissful nights after their wedding. Nights that for him had been full of passion, but for her, full of love.

'Then I must change your mind.' He walked towards her, the bird now settled, and Tiffany stood her ground despite the intent in his eyes. For several long seconds he held her gaze, challenging her, then he turned and walked out of the tent as if she hadn't spoken, as if he didn't want to listen to what she wanted. She followed him out into the hot sun and back to the luxury of the first tent, where the ambiance was far more like the fantasy she'd wanted so much but now needed to resist.

'I'm not going to stay, Jafar, no matter what you do or say.' She stood in the middle of the exotic tent, the aroma of incense mingling with the soft music and the array of colour as gold, red, purple and orange collided around her. A setting far too intoxicating when the man she loved stood in the middle of it. The desert king without a heart.

*But he has my heart.*

'You agreed to stay here, as my wife, for three months.' Jafar's eyes sparked with annoyance but she wouldn't allow him to talk her down. She'd made her decision. She had to leave—for her child's sake.

'Things have changed. I have a baby to consider.'

'Which is why I want you to stay, not for three months as my hired bride, but to remain here as my wife and mother of my child and heir.' He moved towards her, his expression still fierce. Those were words she'd wanted to hear but was he really offering all she'd ever wanted? Worried after the false alarm with his sister, he only wanted the heir she carried because it would keep Shamsumara from Simdan's evil clutches.

'No. I can't. My family…' She began to flounder under the intensity of his eyes, using every excuse she could, except the truth. What would he say if she told him she couldn't stay with him when she loved him, knowing he would never love her?

'In return I will ensure your sister and her child never want for anything again.' His tone was level and devoid of emotion. He was simply brokering another deal with her.

'You want to buy me?' She couldn't believe what she was hearing.

He was making another deal. Putting an offer on the table he knew she would find hard to resist. He might have bought her, but he'd never buy his child, the all-important heir. That required an altogether different currency, one he didn't trade in. Love.

'You brought me here—against my will—and then have the audacity to bribe, or blackmail me, so that I will stay and have your child?'

'It is not like that, Tiffany.' He glared at her, the white of his robes a stark contrast to the colour around them.

'Of course it is. You just want the baby.'

His eyes hardened with the anger of her accusation. 'That is so far from the truth.'

'You told me you never wanted to be a father and that was why you were prepared to even make this stupid marriage deal with me. With your sister's new baby you didn't need an heir, just a bride—a temporary bride.' The agonising hurt of saying the truth out loud almost choked her. She'd only ever been part of a deal. She'd forgotten that and fallen in love with the fantasy she'd been brought to. Worse than that, she'd fallen in love with him.

'It would be against all I believe in, all my people believe in if I allow you to leave Shamsumara knowing you carry my heir.'

'You have your heir.' She was desperate to make him see sense, to realise that forcing her to stay for the baby was even more barbaric than coldly proclaiming he didn't want to be a father.

'I did, but now I have a true heir. One of my own flesh and blood.'

'So what are you going to do? Hold me prisoner? Make me sign another contract—this time for my child?'

'No. This time there will be no contract.' He stepped closer and her heart beat in angry thuds. Or was it because he'd moved too close, because she could smell his unique scent mixed with the desert wind? As she looked into his eyes, into the depths of increasing passion, she knew without a doubt he was going to kiss her—and she wanted him to.

# CHAPTER TWELVE

JAFAR SAW THE fire of desire rise in Tiffany's eyes, turning them into a tumultuous sea of emotion. However much she protested she was far from immune to him, but this wave of passion and desire wasn't what he'd intended. Neither was the kiss he was unable to resist taking. He'd intended to tell her how much he wanted her, how much he wanted their child, that he wanted to create a life with her, a family.

He needed to feel her lips against his, to taste her and crush the softness of her full lips beneath his, but the moment his lips met hers that spark of fire erupted, claiming them both.

She kissed him back, sighing into his mouth as desire drove them harder and higher, sending his plans into disarray. The wild fire of passion scorched him deeper than the desert sun ever could and he knew that whatever the outcome of bringing Tiffany here, he'd never be the same again. He wanted her. Needed her. Loved her.

'It's been too long,' he murmured against her lips as his hands held her arms. He held her close but it wasn't enough. He would never get enough of this woman.

Before she could say anything else, he pulled her against his body, holding her tightly as he kissed her harder, desperate to show what she meant to him, needing to show what he felt for her, but that explosive hot desire erupted once more.

Her tongue danced with his as her body melded against his, her curves moulding to him, fitting perfectly against his body as the haze of desire intensified, taking them to an oasis of sensual pleasure in the middle of the desert. Then it vanished, the desert becoming hostile and barren.

'No.' She pushed him away, shocking him with the force of it. 'This won't change my mind. In fact, all of this is wrong.'

She looked up at him, her breath hard and

ragged. The cream headscarf she'd worn slipped back from her head, exposing the softness of her hair, reminding him how it felt, how it had looked spread out over the pale gold silk of the pillows as he'd made her truly his on their wedding night.

That last thought centred his emotions and he knew that, whatever it took, she would always remain his. 'What is so wrong with a man kissing his wife, Tiffany?'

'I'm not your wife,' she snapped at him and her eyes flashed fiery sparks through the cool darkness of the tent. 'I'm a hired bride. Nothing more.'

The conversation was going wildly off course. He should be kissing her until she wanted nothing but him, until she felt his love for her. But somehow they were still talking about the deal he'd made with her in England. A day that seemed as if it had happened a lifetime ago.

'You were more than that on our wedding night.' He was desperate to remind her of what they'd shared, the passion that had ruled so strongly they'd forgotten even the most basic things. 'That night you became my wife.'

'It's not what I want, Jafar.' A weariness entered her voice and a wave of compassion caught him off guard. 'I don't want passion and desire. I don't want nights filled with steamy sex.'

Her words sent torturous images to his mind, but he maintained his focus, sure that those were just surface words, just as his were. She was protecting herself as much as he was, each refusing to admit what they really felt, what they really wanted. Neither wanting to say the words aloud, each still hiding in the shadows of their past.

He touched his fingers to her face, delicately tracing down the softness of her cheek with the pad of his thumb. The sigh that escaped her as she closed her eyes gave away far more than she thought. It showed the effect he had on her, the need she had for him and, most of all, that her resistance was lowering.

'What do you want, Tiffany?' He kept his tone soft and low.

'I want a man who loves me for who I am, not what I can give him.'

His heart raced as he stood facing the woman who carried his child, the woman he wanted to stay by his side, to be his Queen for ever, but the past still tormented him, still mocked the silly little boy who'd had notions of a long and happy marriage with many children. That little boy had grown up into a cold man, one who only knew how to react to desire or passion, one who'd sworn he never wanted a child to go through what he had and experience being a pawn in a big game plan. He was in line to the throne of Shamsumara and an heir would be expected, but he'd never wanted to create a new life because he had to, because the tradition he'd grown up influenced by demanded it. His sister's pregnancy had created the perfect way out of that and all he'd needed was a temporary bride.

Then he'd married Tiffany, spent an intoxicating night with her and everything had changed. Not because he'd created a child that night. It was far more powerful than that. He'd fallen in love with the woman he'd hired to be his bride.

'You can't do that, can you, Jafar?' Hurt ripped through Tiffany as Jafar stood stoically before her, the passion of his kiss just moments ago gone from his eyes. What cold and heartless plans were going through his mind now?

'You were hired to be my bride, Tiffany—'

'And that is exactly what I have been.' She cut across his words, not wanting to hear the callous truth of why she was here in his desert kingdom.

'But now it's so much more.' He looked into her eyes, a new tenderness filling his, setting light to the torch of hope within her. 'To be here like this was never what I intended.'

The light of hope flickered, threatening to snuff itself out, and she drew on her dwindling reserves of strength to protect her fragile heart. 'It isn't what I agreed to.'

He stroked her hair, then, as if realising he'd stepped over some invisible boundary, let his hand fall back at his side. 'And it isn't what I asked of you.'

'What are we going to do, Jafar?' Her reservoir of determination was sinking ever lower and an unconcealed note of hysteria in her voice was all too clear.

'We have created a new life, a child that will join us together for evermore, no matter where we are or what we do. It was not my intention at all, but it happened and we owe it to our baby to remain together.' She saw his barriers drop, watched as he lowered his guard, but his words still told her the same. He wanted her to stay because of the child she carried.

Memories of the arguments she'd tried not to hear between her parents when she was younger surfaced. Her mother and father had stayed together for Bethany's sake, even going as far as having Tiffany in an attempt to mend the marriage, but it had been a disaster. Just as it would be for her and Jafar.

What they both wanted from the marriage was completely different. She wanted his love, to be able to love him freely. He wanted his heir, to secure the kingdom he'd inherited. Staying together when they were at such polar opposites in their reasons for remaining married would be a disaster. It would be her parents all over again.

'No, Jafar. I can't do that. I can't stay here and I can't be your wife.' The pain in her voice echoed in her heart and for the briefest of seconds she thought she saw it mirrored in his eyes.

'What about your child, *my* son or daughter? They will one day rule Shamsumara.'

She moved towards him, drawn by an unknown force. A need to make him understand forced all her past to the fore, forced out words she'd never admitted out loud to anyone. 'My parents' marriage was not a happy one, Jafar. When my mother fell pregnant with Bethany, they married, as was expected of them by their families.'

'That doesn't mean ours will be unhappy. Our first week of marriage was the happiest I have ever been.'

'It doesn't wipe out the fear I knew as a child when I witnessed angry words between my parents. They didn't love one another. They were forced together when my sister came along.' His dark eyes regarded her as she struggled with ugly memories from her younger years.

'It doesn't mean our marriage will be the same.' His voice was gentle and for a moment she thought he was going to caress her cheek again. Part of her wanted that but part of her knew it would break her heart just a little more.

She continued the story of her past. 'They thought having another baby—me—would bring them closer together. It just pushed them further apart.'

'We have known much pleasure, much passion in our first week of marriage. The kind of passion which brings a man and woman closer to one another emotionally.'

His reference again to their week shut away from the world, the *honeymoon* week, crushed the hope that had started to grow within her. 'But that isn't what I want from you, Jafar.'

There was a sad resignation in her voice as she stood looking up at him. What would he do if she told him she wanted his love? What would he say if she told him she loved him? Maybe saying those words to him was the only way to make him see that their so-called marriage could never work when they both wanted very different things.

'That week was amazing.' She blushed beneath the honesty of her soft words and averted her gaze, anything other than look into the smouldering heat of his eyes as she acknowledged the hot passion that had sparked between them so intensely. 'But it can't sustain a marriage—especially one involving children. I am all too painfully aware of that.'

He lifted her chin with his thumb and finger, forcing her to look at him once more. The heady desire in his eyes was almost too much. 'The passion was, as you say, amazing, but it is not all I want.'

'It isn't?' Her tremulous whisper must surely give away how vulnerable she felt right now. How emotionally exposed.

He shook his head gently. 'No, it isn't. I want

to be loved by the woman who has captured my heart, the woman who takes it soaring across the desert as if on the wings of a falcon.'

He paused and hope flickered to life inside her again. Every barrier he'd erected around himself was stripped away. This was the man she'd fallen in love with. This was the man she'd married and given herself so completely to. A smile lifted her lips at his romantic words and the connection he was making to the bird he'd flown.

'I want to be loved by that woman as much as I love her and, if that is not possible, tomorrow I will let her fly as free as my falcon.'

'You…' Her voice wouldn't work, the words not able to form. Was he really saying he loved her?

He nodded and smiled. 'Yes, Tiffany. My wife, my love. I am madly in love with you and if you leave me my heart will search for yours for ever, miss you for ever. If freedom from me, from being my Queen, is what you desire, then out of love for you I will instruct my plane to take you home.'

* * *

Jafar watched a multitude of emotions play out over his wife's face. Did she believe him? Had he left it too late to finally bear his soul and tell her how much he loved her, how much he wanted her in his life? Even more importantly, could she ever come to love him?

'Jafar,' she said in a husky whisper, a question laced into every syllable, and he closed his eyes, not wanting to hear her rejection, not wanting to know she didn't feel the same, that he'd got it all wrong.

'Yes?' The hesitation, the hope, the raw emotion cracked so sharply in that one word he could hardly comprehend it was his voice. Tiffany looked at him, those lovely blue eyes searching his face, looking for what he didn't know. He hoped it was love, because it must surely be written boldly upon it.

He'd never been this anxious in all his life; never had one person's response mattered so much. Her silence was all too painful and he closed his eyes against the pain of the rejection that was sure to come.

The rejection didn't come. Instead soft lips brushed so lightly over his that he could be imagining it. He opened his eyes and looked right into the blue depths of Tiffany's, immediately lost.

'Your love is all I want from you,' she whispered against his lips, striking up the hum of desire in him. 'My desert fantasy. The man I love with all my heart.'

He took her face in his hands and tenderly kissed her. It was a kiss to show just how much he loved her, but now that he'd broken free of the past it wasn't enough. She'd unlocked the chains that had held his heart and now he was free. Free to love her.

'I love you, Tiffany.' He said it in English, then said it again in his own language, needing to say it aloud as many times as possible.

'I love you, Jafar.'

He smiled at her. 'So my romantic fantasy worked,' he teased her, feeling confident and surrounded by her love.

'This is just the icing on the cake,' she jested, taking his lead. 'The ultimate desert fantasy. An elaborate desert tent and a very sexy sheikh. But it is hearing you say you love me that worked.'

'And so will you stay? Will you be my wife and mother to my child?'

'Until I get a better offer.' So she still teased him, did she?

'In that case—' he swept her from her feet and carried her towards the low and wide bed, adorned with so many vibrantly coloured cushions it was almost camouflaged '—I will have to make sure you never get a better offer.'

'Is that so?' She laughed as he placed her on the softness of the bed.

'It is.' He nodded as he lay next to her, his fingers opening the tie at the front of her dress with ease, revealing her pale skin. 'And I intend to start right now.'

'There will never be a better offer.' Her voice lowered and became soft and serious as she touched her palm to his face. 'Because I love you so much, Jafar.'

He kissed her lips lightly, smoothing her hair from her face and looking into her eyes. 'I love you too, my darling wife.'

# EPILOGUE

*Two years later*

JAFAR WATCHED HIS young son with his older cousin, as they played in the small fountain he'd had installed in the palace gardens. The squeals of delight as the toddlers splashed in the water were infectious; even Leah had abandoned her usual sedate and regal ways to chase around in the garden with the toddlers, barking excitedly as they splashed water at her.

'Our son has his father's leadership qualities,' Tiffany said as she stood beside him under the archway, her hand resting on her stomach and their second child soon to be born. 'Look at him, bossing Zaina around. Poor little girl.'

'I think he might have got that trait from his mother.' As they had done since that night in the desert tent they teased each other, but always with affection.

'I have saved that quality for our little girl.' She looked down at her tummy, at the swell of her second child.

'If she has even half the spirit her mother possesses, she will be a wonderful little girl and I can't wait to meet her.'

Tiffany reached up and touched his face. 'I love you, Jafar. Being here with you is wonderful.'

'You don't miss your old life? Your job?'

Tiffany smiled coyly at the man she was still madly in love with, her ultimate desert fantasy. Did he really question if she missed her old job?

'Bethany is doing a fantastic job running Bridesmaid Services, which means I get to relax and enjoy being an ordinary bridesmaid for Lilly.' She smiled up at him. 'I'm just thankful I will have time to get into the dress after this little one is born.'

His arms pulled her to him, as much as the baby would allow, and he kissed her tenderly. The squeals of laughter increased and they looked out again to see Aaleyah getting carried away with the fun of the water as she too joined in the fun and they laughed, pressing their foreheads together.

'We seem to have a habit of creating unplanned babies.' His sexy voice was full of the memory of the passion they'd shared since that night in the desert.

She blushed prettily and he kissed her lips softly, seductively, promising so much more once they were alone. Her heart soared high into the desert sky, swooping down to find the warm currents of air, and she knew that he had let her fly free that morning after the night of passion and love in the desert. She had been totally free to fly away but she'd chosen the man she loved—and always would.

* * * * *